BILL CONDON's young adult novels *Dogs* (2001) and *No Worries* (2005) were Honour Books in the Children's Book Council Book of the Year Awards. *No Worries* was also short-listed for the Ethel Turner Prize in the 2005 NSW Premier's Literary Awards. *Daredevils* made the long-list in the inaugural Inky Awards, Australia's first teenage choice awards. *Give Me Truth* is Bill's most recent young adult novel for Woolshed Press. Before devoting himself to novels, Bill had a long and successful career as a writer of short stories, plays and poetry for young people. His work encompasses many genres and he has close to one hundred titles to his credit. He lives on the south coast of New South Wales with his wife, the well-known children's author Di (Dianne) Bates.

also by bill condon

Give Me Truth

CONFESSIONS

OF A LIAR, THIEF AND FAILED SEX GOD

bill condon

WOOLSHED PRESS
An Imprint of Random House Australia

A Woolshed Press book
Published by Random House Australia Pty Ltd
Level 3, 100 Pacific Highway, North Sydney NSW 2060
www.randomhouse.com.au

First published by Woolshed Press in 2009

National Library of Australia
Cataloguing-in-Publication Entry

Author: Condon, Bill, 1949–
Title: Confessions of a liar, thief and failed sex god/Bill Condon
ISBN 978 1 74166 454 6 (pbk.)
Target Audience: For children
Dewey Number: A823.3

Cover design by Katherine Barry
Typeset in 11/18 pt Adobe Caslon Pro by Midland Typesetters, Australia
Printed and bound by Griffin Press, South Australia

10 9 8 7 6 5 4 3 2 1

With love to my sisters,
Nanette and Colleen,
and my wife, Di.

1

One huge shiver trudging on to the oval, that's us. First thing on a frostbite Monday morning.

Johnno blows his whistle and we're away. He's Brother John officially, but not to us.

'Jog, boys. That's all I want from you. Nice and easy. Just to limber up.'

I let the main pack go on ahead. Nearly all of our class. I'm waiting for someone and he's late, as usual. That's cool. I'm right at home with the stragglers.

Alan Marshall bobs along, Nick Cleary after him, then Tony Moses, then me, Neil Bridges; single file, freezing cold – bobbing along like a row of shooting gallery ducks.

Seagulls squawk up a storm all around us; having their breakfast or laughing at my dopey running style – it's hard to tell which.

Marshall and Cleary argue about who should have won the weekend footy game; Moses curses the wind for mucking up his hair.

I watch Troy Bosley now, wandering sleepily down the path towards us, taking his own sweet time. He's got a cigarette dangling from his mouth, but he doesn't smoke. Typical Troy act; he likes to push the boundaries, strut the highwire without a net. It's more than just showing off. He can't help it. Troy has his highwire days, but he has nosedives, too. You ask him, he'll tell you straight; he can get crazy.

Smoking's one of the most dangerous things you can do at our school. No one's ever been stupid enough to get caught, but if they did catch you the Brothers would have a great time. After they got through with the strap they'd probably get a couple of heavyweight nuns from the convent to sit on you and squash you to death, to prove smoking is bad for your health.

Now Troy lopes up to Johnno who's standing at his usual place in the centre of the oval.

'Sorry I'm late, Bra. Slept in. Missed the bus. Sorry.'

Johnno has retired from teaching after forty years. That means he started in the 1920s. He must be so ancient. These days he calls himself a potter – 'I potter around, doing a bit of this and that.' Today he's filling in for our real PE teacher, Mr Matthews, who's sick – which doesn't say a lot for PE. Johnno doesn't notice the ciggie burning behind Troy's back; makes no comment about the defiant smirk on his face.

'Not to worry,' he says. 'Off you go with the rest.'

First chance he gets, Troy flicks the butt between Cleary and Marshall.

'Hey!'

'Watch it!'

Grinning, he swaps a high-five with Moses, veers off-course and shoulder-charges me. I dig an elbow into his ribs. He bumps me. I pay him back. We're dodgem cars, bouncing off each other and laughing.

Johnno blows his whistle. He flings his arms about as if he's chasing a swarm of bees.

'You two. Stop that. This instant!'

'Right, Bra.'

We go back to jogging. For a while.

I fix my sights on a tree up ahead.

No need for me to explain the race rules to Troy. We've done this before.

'The gum tree,' is all I say.

As always, I give myself a few steps head start. It's never enough. Troy thrashes me again.

'Aw, real sorry Neil.' He's loving it. 'Did you get lost, mate?'

I have to go through this humiliation and then cop it from Johnno, who's attempting to blow a new hole in his whistle as he hobbles over to us.

He puts on the stern Brother's face because he has to – it's part of the uniform. Doesn't fool us. We all know the whistle's the most dangerous thing about him. He's different from most of the Brothers. They're probably good people deep inside, but it's the outside we see the most. They've got their rosary beads in one pocket and their strap in the other. Strapping and praying, that's what we see.

'Do you boys know what the word "jog" means?' he says.

'Sorry, Bra.'

We hang our heads and look pathetic. It never fails with him.

'Get off with you then.' He gives the whistle another blast. 'On your way. And this time I'll have none of your nonsense.'

Troy unleashes a war whoop. He keeps it going as we set off after the main group. We're not bobbing along now, we're flat-out racing.

The coldness slips away fast and the running makes me feel free. Sometimes I wish that all day long I could just run.

2

Run from school, that's what I'd like to do. It can get you down a bit when it feels like every day is a war and you're always on the losing side. Other than that, life isn't too bad. I have a roof over my head, good parents, a brilliant dog called Dusty, and a brother named Kevin who thinks he's hilarious when really he's just insane.

For instance . . . one night I wander into the bathroom, flip back the toilet lid, unzip my fly – and freeze.

Heavy breathing. It's coming from behind the shower curtain. My pants are zipped up in world-record time. I twist the doorknob but barely get halfway out the door before the shower curtain is flung open.

'Rahhhggghhhh!'

A maniac lunges at me. He's got a raincoat on and knee-high gumboots. And he's holding an axe!

'You bastard!' I scream as I realise who it is.

He's laughing too hard to care.

From the kitchen, Mum calls, 'Take that language outside, Neil.'

'You heard her.' Kevin swings the axe above my head. 'Take your language outside.' Softly he adds, 'Little bastard.'

If there was a game called *Brothers*, leaping out from behind a shower curtain with an axe would have to be a part of it.

'You just wait, Kevin,' I say. 'As soon as you go to sleep, I'm going to get you.'

'Bring it on,' he snarls.

I smile, but I make sure he can't see me.

Kevin is nineteen. I'm three years behind him. Don't think I'll ever catch up.

He's got a motorbike. I've got a bus pass.

He's got his own bank account. I've got my own toothbrush.

He's got Elvis sideburns. I'm secretly using Dad's shaver, but I just scrape off soap.

He's got a girlfriend. I've got several excellent magazines.

The unlucky girl's name is Rose Alexander. When I first heard about her I thought she'd have to be a bottom-of-the-barrel type to go out with Kevin. I was wrong; she's not too bad at all. I think she must have taken pity on him. Sucked in, Rose.

Sometimes I get depressed about not having a girl-friend, but then I remind myself that everyone starts off as a virgin. The trick is not to make a career of it.

Kevin's an apprentice electrician down the mines. He's suited to underground work. The deeper the better, I reckon.

3

My mum and dad work long hours and come home tired. Dad's gone before I wake. He's never bothered to get his driver's licence so it's a 6 am train to the city, and the 5 pm train back home. He's a painter for the Post Office. Pushes a brush around ceilings and walls all week, and on weekends – after we've been to Mass and he's done the yard work – he spends hours out in the shed, painting again, but the kind of thing he likes to do. He calls it doing his Van Gogh impression.

Dad uses anything he can find for a canvas: the back of a sign, a piece of cardboard, or – his favourite – the lids of used ice-cream containers. The shed is full of his masterpieces. Apart from me and Mum and Kevin, no one will ever see them.

It feels sad to me that he can't spend every day doing what he really wants, but Dad just shrugs it away when I tell him that. 'Gotta earn a crust, mate,' he says. 'A man can't live on dreams.'

Mum's the driver of the house. She's also the cleaner, the cook, the chief organiser of everything – 'Boss of the world,' Dad calls her when he's sure she's not listening – and she's the one who does most of the praying. Monday to Friday Mum's out the door by 7 am for her start at National Transformers. It's a factory job, that's all I know. She doesn't talk about it. There's a five-dollar-a-week bonus if she clocks on each day by 7.30. She never misses.

Every night at six we eat dinner at the table – we all take a turn at saying grace – then we clean the dishes and watch TV till 9.30. The reason it's so early is that we have to wash before going to bed. It's Mum's rule. Her father died in his sleep when he was forty-eight. He had dirty feet and Mum's never forgotten it.

Mum goes first: has a fresh tub to herself with all the perfumed bath salts she likes – the smell stinks up every room, there's no escape – and then she pulls out the plug. It's the one luxury she has. Dad has a three-minute shower. I don't think he's real fond of water, but he has another shower in the morning so he's fairly clean for a bloke.

I get the worst fate possible. I have to take the bath after Kevin – using the same water as him. There isn't much hot water left after Mum and Dad have had their turns, so Kevin's bath is always lukewarm. Mine is stone motherless cold. That's because I spend ten minutes before I get in, fishing out the black and curly pubes. I bet Kevin just plucks them off him and sprinkles them all over the bath for fun.

On Saturdays Mum cooks and cleans. She doesn't want any help. 'You'll only get under my feet,' she says. Makes her sound like a water buffalo. I get up early and walk Dusty for an hour or so. I let her off into the marshes at the creek and she goes fossicking after rabbits. She's got no chance of catching one – just as well too, she wouldn't know what to do with it. When I get home again I work outside with Dad. Kevin used to help us but he's got Rose now. Dad mows the lawn and I do the edges. It's probably not much to anyone else, but it means a lot to me when he says I've done a good job.

Dad always finishes up with a glass of home-brew – only the one each week. He pours me a shandy, but the older I get, the more he cuts back on the lemonade. His grog is rough as guts, but I never complain. It's good to be able to share something with him.

Every Saturday night Mum writes in the huge old family journal, jotting down everything we did during the week. It was her father's journal too, and before that her grandfather's. 'One day,' she says, 'it'll be yours.' I hate it when she talks like that.

Sundays we go to church. Kevin's given up on that, too. Mum is right into religion, and Dad backs her up. I make all the right noises at the right times, but I'm not really sure about anything. It would be different if you could actually see God, instead of having to take everyone's word that He's around. I suppose it's just a matter of hanging in there. Maybe one day I'll walk into a church, and God'll be there for me, clear as day.

4

When I'm not at home with my family I'm off somewhere with Troy. He lives two streets behind me. Half a mile on from his place is Bottle Brush Creek. It's all stinking mudflats when the tide is out but when it's in we go fishing and hunting around the banks for blue-tongue lizards. One time we made a canoe out of sheets of corrugated iron tied together with wire.

Troy was sure it was going to float. I told him there wasn't a chance.

We both agreed on one thing: last one to abandon ship was chicken.

As soon as it hit the water the canoe began its Titanic imitation. That's when I bailed out and scrambled to dry land. Troy rode it till it sank beneath the surface. I always end up being chicken. It's hard not to be when you're up against Troy. He doesn't know how to back down.

* * *

The railway bridge is built over the creek. That's where we are today.

'I've got an idea,' he says. 'You game, Neil?'

'Depends what it is.'

'So you're not game?'

'You wish,' I tell him. 'I'm more game than you – no matter what it is.'

I follow him along a rough and narrow track that leads us under the bridge – under the tracks.

'Yeah, this is perfect,' he says. 'Watch this.' He shoves his head up in the gap between two sleepers. 'Fanntastic! Give it a go, Neil!'

'Are you mad? What if a train comes?'

He drops back down next to me. 'That's the whole idea, bird brain. We stick our heads up when a train's comin'. First one to move is chicken. You still game?'

No, I'm not. It's too dangerous. It's ridiculous.

But then I see this smart-alecky grin creep over his face as if he knows he's got me.

'Sure,' I tell him. 'Let's do it.'

We wait there looking down the track for a good fifteen minutes and then we see the red rattler curl around a bend.

'Make sure you've got plenty of room to duck back down,' Troy warns. 'Wouldn't want to get your head stuck – might hurt.'

'You worry about your own fat head,' I say.

Here comes the rattler. Two or three hundred yards off yet.

Troy waves out to the driver, who sees him and blows the train whistle long and loud; keeps blasting it all the way along the track.

I'm not going to be the chicken this time. But neither is Troy.

A hundred yards.

It isn't slowing down.

Fifty yards.

Bugger it – I'm the chicken.

I dive for cover and a split second later so does Troy.

A thousand tons of train rumble above us.

And then –

Errggh! Yuck! Yuck! Yuck!

Troy almost splits his face, he's laughing so hard.

Someone went to the toilet on the train.

I got peed on!

'It's not funny, Troy.'

'It is from where I'm standin'.'

I wash my face and hair in the creek and Troy gives me his shirt when I throw mine away.

'Go on, admit it,' he says. 'It was fun.'

All the years I've known Troy it's been like this. I tag along behind him and I usually end up getting into trouble. Sometimes I even get peed on. But like I say to him, 'It's always fun.'

5

My life is neatly divided into two halves: home and school. There's nothing else.

Today it's school.

I'm sitting at my desk when I hear shouting in the quadrangle. Everyone swivels around to look out the windows. Our teacher, Mr Harris, is too busy having a good gawk himself to stop us from watching. We see two figures: Brother Mick, the Principal, and Zom Zeeba, who's in the same class as me.

No one's seen anything like this before. Zom swings wild punches. Mick can't get close enough to stop him. Broad daylight. Middle of the quad. A kid fighting a Brother – fighting the Principal. For a second I wonder if I'm dreaming it. Every one of us would love to knock Mick's teeth out. We're all too gutless – except for Zom. He's the last one anyone would expect it from. He's slow and sleepy-looking; plays the violin; chess is his favourite sport. Plenty make fun of him but he smiles it off. He's a loner and it fits him. I've never thought much about Zom at all, but if I had, I'd have seen him as being like me, another grey dot in the background. He's more than that.

Mick reminds me of a gnarly old tree, tall and tough; run up against him, you die. It's almost like two against one. He tackles Zom and wrestles him down. Drives a knee into his back. A few in our class shudder and moan as if they can feel the knee crunching into them. A few more murmur: threats and curses. Mick hauls Zom to his feet. The fight's nearly all blown out of Zom now. He staggers as Mick pins his arm behind his back and half-marches, half-drags him across the quad.

When Zom tries to pull away Mick cranks the arm up higher. Zom roars out his pain and anger. His voice rises louder and louder until clear across the school all we hear is the word *fuck*. He keeps on saying it, wailing it. It's like a one word language that expresses everything he feels. No one swears at our school. At least not loud enough for the Brothers to hear. You'd have to be out of your mind to do that.

Mick bellows back at him. It's an animal noise, nothing human. He takes Zom by the shoulders and shakes him, screaming into his face. Then he shoves him backwards and Zom stumbles around, reaching out, trying to find something to hold him up. He loses his balance and down he goes. A dozen classrooms circle the quad and from every one of them erupts the sound of pit-bull boys booing and shouting their hate.

The quad is suddenly full of swirling black habits that look like frenzied, wing-flapping birds; the Brothers running, their voices charging ahead of them: 'Stop! Stop! Noooo!'

Zom rolls himself into a ball as Mick stands over him poised to kick.

Mr Harris slams his cane against the wall. 'RETURN TO YOUR SEATS!' He grabs Stuart Whitmarsh by the scruff of the neck and heaves him towards his desk. Kennedy and Tukac get the same treatment. 'The show is over! Sit down – and do it QUIETLY!'

Harris rushes from window to window dropping the blinds with a crash so we can't see anything. But we've already seen it and it's never going to go away.

6

It's the only thing we talk about at the first break from class, replaying every scene like last night's best TV show. Simon Portelli is the star reporter. Before the action spilled into the quad there was an argument outside the Science block. Simon saw the whole thing.

'Mick starts goin' off at Zom about stealin' a wallet when we got changed for PE. Zom doesn't have a clue. He's like, "What wallet? What are you talking about?" Mick says, "You're a liar, son! A liar and a thief!"'

Portelli pauses to grab a fresh breath. His eyes dart around like a jittery animal at a waterhole. No Brothers nearby, so he launches himself into it again.

'You know how red in the face Mick gets? Well, it's like he's on fire this time. Completely loses it. Pushes Zom up against the wall. Jabbin' his finger into his chest. Keeps on at him – "Admit it, boy! You stole that wallet! Admit it! Admit it!" And when he doesn't, that's when Mick punches him. In the gut. Closed fist. Full on. Hard as he bloody can!'

After school, outside the gates, Zom slumps on the concrete with his back against the brick fence. He must have been sitting there for hours, waiting for us to come out. Still in his school uniform. Blood spattered on his white shirt. A group gathers around throwing questions at him. The fire that he had in the quad has vanished. He's the soft-voiced no one again, the chess player thinking through every word as though it's an important move. He speaks without any anger, without any feeling at all. It's as if he's describing someone else's fight, one that he's seen from a great distance.

I stop to listen but Troy doesn't want to be there. He squirms and fidgets before he nudges me, mouthing, 'Let's go.' I stay long enough to hear Zom fill in the only blank I wasn't sure about.

'I got expelled.' He shrugs. 'Just like that. All because of something I didn't even do.'

Troy edges away and I follow him. I'm the only one who knows what he's feeling. We're well clear of the others before he speaks.

7

'Christ, Neil. It wasn't supposed to be like that.'

'I know.'

'I don't even know why I did it.'

All I can do is nod as I think back to this morning. We'd just finished our exercise routines down in the huge old tin shed the Brothers call a gym. Most of the class was already on the way back to school but there were a few lagging behind, slow to change from their white shorts and T-shirts back into their uniforms.

Troy and I were there. We both saw Paul Burke drop his wallet on a bench. He had his back turned and was bent over, tying up his shoelaces. It took about one second for the wallet to disappear. Troy nodded towards the door and took off. I went with him, not sure what was going on. At first I thought he was only mucking around, thought he'd dangle the wallet in front of Burkie and say, 'Hey, look what I found' – something like that. But he got out of there fast and never looked like stopping. Zom blundered towards Burkie as we walked out. Just in time to be the prime suspect.

'I never knocked anything off before, you know that, right?'

'Sure, I do, Troy.'

'It was crazy. I dared myself to do it. It was so friggin' dumb!'

'Hey, Troy. It's okay. You can still fix this.'

'You think so? How?'

'Simple. Tomorrow you hand the wallet in to Brother Mick, that's how. Say you found it.'

'Aw, sure. It's that easy.'

'It is!'

'Yeah, and he'll know straightaway I took it.'

'How will he?'

'Where you been, Neil? Wake up! One look at my face and he'll know! They always know!'

'All right. Fine. But you have to do *something*. Sneak into his office. Leave it on his desk – you gotta get Zom out of this.'

'You think it'll change anything? He took a swing at a Brother. I can't get him out of that. No one can.'

'You can try.'

'Just shut up about it, will ya? Leave it alone. Leave me alone. I don't want to talk about it.'

He only takes a few shaky steps before he turns to face me.

'I know what I should do,' he says. 'And I wish I could. But I just can't. All right? It's too big now, Neil. All I want is to forget it ever happened. You can understand that, can't you?'

In my mind maybe there's some hesitation, but I don't let Troy see it. He's my best friend.

'Yeah.' I walk on with him. 'I understand. It was just bad luck. Zom'll be all right . . .'

Even as I say it I doubt that it's true.

'Thanks, Neil. I owe ya.'

Troy pulls the wallet out of his pocket and chucks it into the bushes beside the road. I see it land, the money untouched and jutting out from inside it. One lousy five dollar note.

8

I have this annoying problem that gives me a lot of trouble: a conscience. All afternoon it gnaws away, nibbling at my thoughts. After I leave Troy I decide to go the long way home – past Zom Zeeba's house. I don't want to do it. I hate the idea. But I don't think I've got a choice. I'm never going to tell Troy I did this. He might think it's some kind of double-cross. It's not. No way am I going to mention that wallet. I just think I should check on Zom, let him know that someone has his back – even if only for a little while. I'll spend five minutes with him at the most, so he knows that he's not alone, and then I'll go.

It sounds like a phony baloney exercise, I know, but I only want to cheer him up, I'm not signing on to be his best mate. Five minutes – in and out – and my conscience will be clear.

* * *

The door is opened with a whoosh, as if someone is trying to pull it off the hinges. In front of me is a short and chunky man; no hair on his head but plenty of it – grey and matted – on his bare chest.

His way of saying hello is a glare.

I tell him I'm a friend of Ray's – that's Zom's real name. I don't get any further than that.

'Raymond no live here no more. You see him at he sister's place. He disgrace. For himself, the family – disgrace. You know about this?'

It takes me a moment to assemble my thoughts – this has to be Zom's father – he's so full on he rattles me.

'Um, yeah,' I say. 'If you mean about the fight with Brother Michael. Yeah, I know about that. The whole school saw it.'

'Bloody. Bloody. You no hit man of God. You no hit man of God and live in my house!'

He's fired up and ready to attack. I don't like to contradict him, but I have to.

'It wasn't Ray's fault,' I say, too feebly. 'Brother Mick – the Principal – he was belting into him. Ray fought back, that's all. He didn't do anything wrong.'

'No? You think? Nothing wrong? Are you joke me? He hit man of God! You understand? Huh? Is disgrace!'

I take a step back so I'm out of his punching range. I want to tell him that Mick isn't a man of God, he's a bully and a dickhead. But I decide it's best to keep that information to myself.

'You want see Raymond?' His eyes are intense and furious. 'You go see he sister. Sylvana. Raymond there. I threw out. Out of my house! He no good!'

He stomps inside and slams the door.

Well, that was interesting. I've just been blown away by the human version of a cyclone. So that's where Zom got his fighting spirit from. Or his crazy streak. I feel relieved to be getting out of it all. I did my best. Copped a blast for my trouble. Okay, conscience, now you can go back to sleep. Yes, I feel sorry for Zom. He gets beaten up by a Brother, then expelled, then kicked out of home. I hope he's okay, but it's not my problem anymore.

'Wait. Please. You wait.'

I spin around and see a woman hurrying towards me. She's built wide and close to the ground. It's Zom's mum, for sure.

'You are Raymond friend?' she asks.

Zom hasn't got any enemies – he lopes along content in his own headspace – but he hasn't got any real friends either. I'd rather his mum didn't find that out – not from me at least.

'I'm sort of his friend. My name's Neil.'

For an awful second I think she's going to hug me, but she makes do with a very grateful smile.

'You forgive my Mario? Yes? I sorry. He upset today.'

'Sure.'

'Is what he was taught – the Church. You must honour. You know? Is terrible what happened Raymond. "Out of my house!" Mario say. "Out of my house!" He no listen me, no listen Raymond. Holy Mother! Is terrible.'

'I wish I could help you . . . but anyway – good luck. Let Ray know that Neil said hi. Okay?'

As if I haven't spoken at all, she says, 'Number 23.'

'Right . . . what about it?'

'Morton Street? You know this one?' She points down the road.

'I know it.'

'Number 23, unit 8; my Sylvana's flat. Raymond, he with her. You go see Raymond now? Yes?'

I want to tell her that I can't do it but she's looking at me with so much hope.

Oh well. It's not much further to walk.

'Yeah. Of course I'll see him. While I'm here. Might as well.'

9

Unit 8 is perched on the top of four steep and twisty flights of stairs. A striped orange cat is parked outside the door like a furry doormat. I knock and hear footsteps inside. Locks are turned and the door opens. The cat darts in.

'Yes?'

A girl. She's probably in her early twenties. Way too old for me. She's pretty.

'Hi. My name's Neil Bridges. I was told that Ray Zeeba lives here. I'm in his class at school.'

'Ah.' She pokes her head back into the flat. 'Raymond. You've got a visitor.' And then she looks at me again, half smiles and opens the door wider. 'Come in.'

She's *very* pretty. I can't help but stare. Her dark eyes bore straight in to me. They stay there for three seconds, tops, before she looks away. Only three seconds but it's still a record. Girls don't usually bother to look at me at all. When they do I see a message flashing in their eyes that suggests now would be a good moment for me to drop dead. I don't get that this time. I see question marks. I feel she wants to know who I am, what I'm like. I have the same questions about her, but I don't think I'll ever find out the answers. Girls like her, they're way out of my reach.

She bustles ahead to scoop some clothes off the only chair that I can see. It's in front of the TV set. There's no other furniture. The room is small and stale.

'Raymond! What are you doing? Someone's here to see you. Come on.' She turns back to me. 'He won't be long. I think he was having a shower.'

'There's no rush.'

'I'm Sylvie. Raymond's – Ray's sister. He's staying with me for a while. Did you say your name was –'

'Neil – Bridges. Hi.'

'Hi, Neil.'

She puts out her hand and I hold it for a second too long, in some kind of first hand-holding trance, before I snap out of it and shake it as if it's just an ordinary hand.

'Did you hear about the problem Ray had at school?'

'I saw it happen. That's why I'm here. Wanted to know if he's okay.'

'That's nice of you.'

'I'm amazed that his dad kicked him out.'

'Yes, Dad can be a handful. Ray and I both love him to death but he's got some very old-fashioned ideas. I couldn't live up to his expectations either. I'm afraid I'm not the good Italian girl Dad was hoping for . . .'

Zom appears in the hallway, drying his hair after the shower.

'Ah, here he is,' Sylvie says, 'at last. You've got company, Ray.'

'Aw, Neil.' He gives me a nod. 'I didn't expect to see you here.'

He's got a curved red mark in the shape of a comma under one eye and his top lip is puffy.

'Thought I'd check up on you,' I tell him. 'See if you've booked a rematch with Mick.'

He grins at that – reminds me of a big shaggy dog wagging his tail.

Sylvie walks to the door. 'I'm ducking down to the shop – we need some bread and milk. I'll leave you two to talk. Good to meet you, Neil.'

'You too.'

Her smile has warmed up. That first one she found for me was cautious. The latest is friendly and welcoming. I wish it was more than that.

10

Zom runs a hand through his brown jungle of hair. His hair's always like that, and he's usually got his shirt half hanging out, the way it is now. Some blokes come packed and ready for life; some are like Zom.

'I'm glad you came.' He squats down on the floor and I do the same. 'I haven't heard from anyone else at school. I don't suppose I will.'

I let that go past without a comment. But he's got it right. Most of the blokes in our class have a laugh at Zom's expense – I'm no exception. He gets singled out because he's backward in some things. I don't mean dumb or retarded. It's more that his thoughts take a while to drop into place. He thinks everything through – he's big on pondering. You tell a joke and he's usually the last one to get it. It could be because he wasn't born here and he's grown up with other kinds of jokes than the ones we tell. Or maybe Zom just listens and ponders because that's what smart people do. I don't know what it is with him – but he's different to us.

A few kids in our class saw *The Night of The Living Dead* and they came back to school the next day with his nickname: Zom, short for Zombie. They reckoned he was like one of the walking dead, the way he lurched along in a brain fog. He didn't mind it. Big joke to him. Insults bounce off Zom and never seem to leave a mark. He's like Superman for the Nerd team.

When you get someone like that, and you throw in hobbies like chess and playing the violin, well, he'd better like his own company.

'How did you know to come here?' he asks.

'Your mum gave me the address. I saw your father first. He's a piece of work, that bloke – almost took my head off.'

'Sorry, Neil.'

'Doesn't matter. He told me what happened. Kicking you out. That's a low act. Didn't he see how your face was cut up by Mick?'

'That didn't mean anything to him.' He shrugs. 'I understand how he thinks. It's black or white with him. No in-between. I hit a Brother. It doesn't matter *why* I did it.'

'But he'll come around after a while, don't you reckon? Let you go back home?'

'No. Not my father.'

Without emotion, that's how he says it – flat – like it's a cold, textbook fact. After what's happened to him today, I think maybe he hasn't got any emotion left in him.

He sinks down into himself then. I'm sitting so close to him, but he feels like he's off somewhere on another planet. He picks at a thread in the carpet – lost in thought – or just plain lost.

'You okay there, Zom?'

He takes a second or two to stir . . .

'I'm fine . . . trying to put things together, that's all – this stuff keeps going around in my head – about Brother Michael.'

'What about him?'

'If I tell you, can it be just between us?'

'Yeah, Zom, just between us.'

'Well, I know I'm supposed to forgive him, but I don't think I can. I'm pretty sure I never will.'

'So? That's only natural after what he did to you. You're angry.'

'No. I'm over being angry. I don't care about what he did to me. It's what he did to my family, and what he'll do to the next family.'

'What are you saying, Zom?'

'Brother Michael isn't getting away with this.'

'Yeah? What are you going to do?'

'I'm not sure yet.'

'I wouldn't mind seeing his letterbox get blown up. I've got some double bungers at home. They're all yours if you want 'em.'

He pauses, soaks up what I said, then shakes his head.

'No. If this is going to be done, then it should be done properly. I want to stop him. Completely.'

Most blokes make a big noise when they talk about getting even with the Brothers. They're full of rage – shouting and swearing – I've heard it before. Every time it turns out that the big noise is all they've got. There's nothing behind their threats and they fizzle out in a few days or a week – and the Brothers carry on doing what they like.

Zom hasn't made any noise at all. I believe what he's saying. Whether it happens or not is something else, but just the fact that he's considering it makes me feel bad. Troy and that wallet have brought him to this, and I've played a part in it – me and my silence.

'Go, Zom!' Big smile. False laugh. 'You get him.'

For once he doesn't smile back.

I see his violin in a corner and stand up to have a closer look. Any excuse to change the subject. He follows me over to it.

'You want to play something for me, Zom?'

'I don't think so. Sorry, Neil. I only took it up because my father wanted me to. It made him happy. I didn't think I'd like it, but I really do. But I can't play it now. I'm not going to play it till I see him again – however long that takes.'

I make my way to the door. Zom walks with me, squeezing in some answers to questions I should have asked.

'I'm not going to look for another school,' he says. 'I was leaving at the end of this year anyway. I'll get a job; anything at all. I have to help Sylvie pay for food, pay my share of the rent – I want to get my own place as soon as I can.'

'Good luck with it.' I step outside. 'Let me know how things go. I'm in the phone book. All right?'

'Thanks, Neil. I'll do that.'

I get the feeling I'll never hear from him again.

I leave him with a punch on the shoulder and a final grin.

'See ya.'

Conscience time is over.

11

I wind down the steps and catch Sylvie on the ground floor about to head back up.

'Did it go okay?' she asks.

'Yeah, fine.'

'I'm really grateful that you're looking out for Ray.' She glances up the stairwell to make sure we're alone. 'You never know what's going on inside with him. Did he say anything, about what happened at school?'

Just between us.

Have to stick to it.

'Not really. He doesn't say much to me either.'

'Well, he might one day – now that he knows he has someone he can talk to.'

I feel like I should put her straight but I don't know how to go about it. I'm umming and ahhing when she suddenly leans into me – and kisses my cheek.

'Thanks, Neil. For caring.'

All I can do is stare at her. My face instantly burns

with redness. I know a kiss on the cheek is not meant to be anything out of the ordinary, but it's never happened to me before. With my mum, yeah – but this is a real girl. This is a woman.

'Do you live far away?' she asks.

She's not just pretty. She's beautiful.

'No, not far. Joyce Street. It's on the other side of the highway – 11 Joyce Street. Twenty minutes' walk, that's all. If you're ever going by you're welcome to call in.'

'Thanks for that. Do you think you might come back here again – to see Ray?'

'Yeah, I will for sure – definitely!'

I say it with too much passion, too much need. And then, so there can be no mistaking that I'm an idiot, I say it again.

'You can count on it – there'll be a next time!'

A smile flickers around the corners of her mouth – is she happy or just amused? 'I'll look forward to it.'

One last smile and she walks up the stairs without looking back.

For a few minutes on the way home I manage to hypnotise myself.

You're a sex god, Neil. Sylvie wants your body. That kiss was a big hint. Go for it!

37

Then I think of her age and I snap out of it. She must be about twenty-two or twenty-three. It's not only that she's too old; she's way too classy for me in every way. She needs someone who's sexually cool. I can't order chicken breasts in a shop without blushing. Reluctantly, I have to admit there was nothing at all to the kiss, apart from her being nice. I sigh long and deep and store Sylvie way up at the back of my mind with all my other fantasies, in a box marked Impossible.

12

A day goes past, then three. School is back to normal. Every sign of Zom swept away like he never was. All traces of rebellion squashed. We're back in our cages again, too afraid to roar.

Today, the same as every second Friday, we're marshalled into a snaking line that leads us two-by-two up the hill and over the white wooden bridge that separates us from the girls' school.

Any boy caught crossing the bridge without permission in order to feel up, perve on, or do something equally wicked to the girls will be crucified.

No Brother has ever said those words to us but we all know that's exactly what they mean. We'd have to be deaf and dumb not to know – they've been beating us over the head with it since we started at the school when we were nine or ten.

The only day we're legally allowed to cross the bridge is today. That's when we go to confession at Sacred

Heart, a church located slap-bang in the middle of Saint Brigid's school grounds. Brother Clementian watches our every move, of course, but it's still like a tiny wander through Heaven.

Saint Brigid's girls wear long and flowing uniforms of steel that reach to their ankles. At that point white socks take over guard duty to ensure that not the slightest morsel of bare skin is available for the ogling pleasure of deviants such as me. These uniforms were designed with the specific intention of driving boys berserk . . . lucky we've all got dazzling imaginations.

'Eyes straight ahead, boys,' commands Clementian. It's like he's gone sticky-beaking into our minds and seen what we're thinking. 'You should be concentrating on what you are going to say to Father. Don't waste this opportunity. Make it a good confession.'

We walk past an open door and I see girls my age. Beautiful girls. Singing. It's not the barbed-wire noise boys crank out. It's sweet and smooth, just like the silky skin on a girl's body . . . it's amazing how excited I can get without even trying. Putting the words *silky*, *skin* and *body* in the same sentence is hazardous, for me at least. My thoughts cause what can best be described as a sudden growth spurt. It's not my fault, it's hormones. I might need to see a doctor because I think I have my share of them and someone else's as well.

Troy nudges me, a dirty smirk on his face. I think I've been sprung, but he isn't looking at me.

He points ahead of us. 'Check out Bails.'

Three rows up I see that Warwick Bailey has the same problem as me. He does his best to ignore it, but then falls out of line for a few seconds because it's tricky to walk and he needs to make an adjustment. Tell me about it.

'Mr Bailey!'

Clementian is right onto him.

'Yes, Bra?'

'What are you doing, boy?'

'Nothing, Bra.'

'Then get your hands out of your pockets before you do nothing again! And pull up your socks!'

'Yes, Bra.'

'It's not too hard for you, is it?'

'Yes, Bra.'

'What?'

'No, Bra.'

Clementian swaggers off as everyone laughs and sniggers at Bailey. We're all saying, 'What a loser,' but we're thinking, 'Lucky it wasn't me who got caught.' I close my eyes and I can see the girls singing angelically, without clothes on. I don't do it on purpose, which is one good thing, but I can't stop looking, which is equal to two bad things.

The hormones cause me to remember Sylvie and that kiss she planted on me. She hasn't got any clothes on either. The difference between her and the schoolgirls is that we've talked, I've held her hand, she's kissed me. It's too much for me. Just by thinking about her, I'll go blind on the spot. I force myself to concentrate on something else, like an old lady's blue and bulgy legs, like the smell of cabbage cooking on the stove, or Mum serving up tripe for Dad's dinner. I manage to push Sylvie away but I know I'll bring her back later, when I'm alone. Sorry, God.

13

Today there are two confessionals operating. On the left side of the church about thirty kids sit in pews, all waiting to have their confessions heard by Father Collins. He's fairly young, fresh out of priest school. Tall and strong as any footy player. What I like most is that he jokes around, and lets us call him Jim. It makes him flesh and blood.

On the right side of the church there are just a few waiting for Father O'Brian to hear their confessions. They must all have a death wish. O'Brian is an old crank. So many times I've heard him yelling at kids. He's famous for it.

'Don't you lie to me, boy! You do that and you slap God across the face!'

Goes over real big with your classmates when O'Brian's voice crashes around the rafters. Fruit loop.

* * *

Three of us have a pew to ourselves, me and Troy and Bails.

'Glad I'm seein' Jim,' Bails whispers to me.

'Me too. They ought to retire that O'Brian.'

He keeps his head low so Clementian can't see us.

'Drop him off a cliff, be better,' he fires back.

'Feed him to the sharks,' mutters Troy.

'Nooo.' Bails grins. 'He'd poison 'em.'

Bails can't stop a laugh from escaping; just one short machine-gun cackle.

The sound is too big for church.

'Shhhhh!'

Clementian appears, prowling up and down the aisle. He's short with slick oily hair, white as chalk. I haven't seen him in the dark but I wouldn't be surprised if his hair glowed like some kind of alien. He's probably only in his twenties, but he has a granite face, as if he was born already old and sour. I don't think he could crack a smile to save his life.

He stops in front of our pew. His eyes burn a hole through my head. I kneel down as if I'm praying. Troy and Bails join me. They can't touch you if you're praying. I hope. You really never know for sure with Clementian. Unable to stop it, my mind screens a re-run of him grabbing Gregor Jozwiak by the shirtfront and dragging him out of his seat because he laughed. It's a Mortal Sin to laugh in Clementian's class.

I'm back in the day when it happened, watching it in real time as Jozwiak is flung against a fibro wall, smashing a gaping hole in it. He lies on the ground face down. Clementian roars for us to get back to our work. Jozwiak doesn't move. It's only five or so seconds before his head comes up and he looks around him, but time never took so long.

Clementian's still glaring. Deciding.

And now here he comes.

We're done for, until, at exactly that moment, Father O'Brian storms out of his confession box.

'You boys!' He points at the mob waiting to see Jim. 'I want half of yer over here to take confession with me! Right this minute! Move!'

Troy and Bails clamber over each other to be ahead of the pack and avoid Clementian. I'm right beside them. It's not too hard because no one else is exactly in a hurry to meet and greet the priest from Hell. He's a better bet than Clementian, that's all I care about. He doesn't pack a strap.

We have some waiting time before our confessions roll around. Bails chomps his nails and flips the shrapnel at the line of heads in front of us.

Troy sits with his arms folded tight against his chest as if he's keeping his heart held prisoner. I wish he was seeing Jim instead of O'Brian. Maybe then he could talk about the wallet . . . on second thoughts, he wouldn't even then. Nearly all of us are the same. I don't know if it's guilt or fear of the strap, but our secrets never see daylight.

Finally it's my turn. O'Brian slides the window open that separates us. I make the sign of the cross and then parrot the words: *'Bless me, Father, for I have sinned. It is two weeks since my last confession.'*

I don't know what to say next. If I'd had more time I would have made up some lies. I have plenty of true material to draw from – like punching Kevin while he was asleep and swearing black and blue to Mum and Dad that I didn't do it; like standing in front of a mirror and taking a photo of myself in the nude with that new instant camera Dad got for Christmas, then weighing the camera down with a brick and throwing it into the river because my photo got stuck inside it; like knowing the truth about the nicked wallet. But I'm not telling O'Brian my real sins. Fat chance. I think everyone seeing him today is going to lie. Confession is supposed to leave you free of sin and spotless of soul. Not the way we do it. It's more likely that the lot of us will burn in Hell.

'Well then, boy? I'm waitin' for yer.'

'I missed Mass, Father.'

'You WHAT?'

Terrific. They must have heard that in China.

'Talk to me, son. Why did yer miss Mass?'

'Sorry, Father – I forgot.'

'Oh, well that's all right then, if yer forgot, I beg your pardon – it's not a problem at all.'

He likes to build your hopes up.

'My good fellow –'

Here it comes.

'Do yer know what happens when yer forget God?'

'No.'

'He forgets you! And when God forgets you, it's Hell on Earth! Hell on Earth! Is that what yer want?'

'No, Father.'

'Then straighten yerself out! Yer with me there, lad?'

'Yes, Father.'

'For your penance say six decades of the rosary.' He rattles a prayer of absolution at me. He could be gargling for all I know. 'Send in the next boy.' The window slams shut.

I kneel down, like you're supposed to do after confession, but I don't say the penance. I reckon it's enough just having to go in and face O'Brian. I'm not completely against praying, but I'd rather keep it for an emergency.

14

Troy is in with O'Brian for only a few minutes before he saunters out and joins us again. He rolls his eyes as he kneels down and pretends to pray. I guess that he's been given a hard time so I mime a belly laugh. You get good at mime when you go to our school. The Brothers don't know they're teaching it, but every time they strap someone for talking in class or at church, our mime skills improve out of sight.

'Hey,' I nudge him, 'whatcha say to him?'

'Same as you.' He looks down to his hand, thumb and forefinger curled into a zero.

After the last confession is heard we file out of the church and drift back to school. When Clementian is far enough away, Bails tell his story.

'That O'Brian, he was trying to get me to be a priest.'

Troy laughs. 'That's a classic.'

'Would be,' I say, 'if it was true.'

'Deadset, Neil. He was telling me what a great life it was and how it was the best way to serve God. They have someone who does their cleanin' and cookin' and everything. It sounded pretty all right to me.'

'What did you say, Bails?'

'I asked him if I could bring me dog.'

'You what?'

'Ye-ah! I'm not leavin' me dog for anyone.'

Troy turns to me, grinning like it's the funniest thing he's ever heard. What makes it even funnier is that we know Bails is deadly serious.

'And can you?' Troy keeps a straight face.

'Nah. He said no dogs are allowed, so I told him, no thanks.'

'Bails, you're a dickhead.'

Troy and I say it together, as if we've been rehearsing it all our lives.

'What did I do?' he asks. 'What did I do?'

And that cracks us up even more.

School can be a hard place when the teachers go mental on you. Then one of us will say something just plain stupid and it'll be like this and we're laughing and no strap is big enough to hurt us.

15

I'm back at home, walking past the phone one afternoon when it calls out to me, almost like it knew I was there.

I snatch it up, thinking it's Troy.

'Yep?'

'Hello, Neil. It's Sylvie. Ray's sister.'

I gulp first. Then I try to come up with something incredibly witty to say, but I don't have the hour or so it would take.

'Hi. What's happenin'?'

'I have some good news for you.'

Wild and crazy thoughts stir inside me. I'm an optimist when it comes to sex.

'What is it?'

'Well, for a start, Ray's got his own place now. It's only one room but he likes it there. Isn't that great?'

Is that all? Who cares?

'Yeah, it is. That's really terrific news.'

'Yes – but the best thing is – he's got a job!'

Come on, Neil. Get some enthusiasm going here.

'Cool! That's so good. What's he doing?'

'He's an usher at the Vista.'

'Okay.'

'I thought you'd want to know that things are finally going right for him – he was so down that day you visited.'

'I do – I'm glad you told me. I've been wondering what he's up to.'

'He only started yesterday. I can't wait to check out his uniform. He has to wear a bow tie and a red vest – he's going to hate it.'

'I reckon. I should go there and stir him up a bit – throw some popcorn at him.'

'Well now, there's a thought. I'm seeing him today. I said I'd drop off some keys. You could meet me there if you like. I'm not sure about the popcorn, but we could tease him a little bit. I'm going to stay on and watch the movie. You're welcome to join me.'

I stare at the phone. Did she really say that? She wants me to go to a movie with her?

'Neil?'

God. She thinks I've fainted.

'I'm here. And yes, count me in – for both. I'll check out Ray and his bow tie – and I'd love to see the movie. You say when and I'll be there.'

'Fabulous. Now is good. I've just finished my shift. I can be there in half an hour.'

'Half an hour. I can do that ... not a problem. The Vista it is.'

16

'Yes!'

I rush through the house, throwing off my school uniform as I go. Into the shower for a one-minute wonder wash. Brush teeth. Comb hair. Check out the mirror – it screams and tells me to put some clothes on. Clothes on. Check out the mirror – it still screams. All this in fifteen minutes. My fastest time ever.

I fall out of the house and onto the street, doing up buttons – oh yeah, and my zipper – shoelaces can wait. Now where's the bus? I look at my watch and realise it left ten minutes ago. I start running. I'm going so fast, I'm burning. I'm flying. But I'm still going to be so late. My first date and I'm not even going to be there for it.

Then a miracle flashes towards me. Kevin on his motorbike. I leap in front of him and hope he doesn't run me down.

He stops. And swears at me.

'Sorry, Kevin. It's an emergency. I need a ride.'

He swears at me again.

'I'll never ask you for another favour as long as I live, if you just do this one thing for me.'

'Why should I?'

'I'm your brother.'

'And?'

'I have to meet a girl at the Vista. It's really important. I've never met a girl before – anywhere . . .'

He keeps on looking angry.

'Kev, I'll be your slave. I'll clean your side of the room. I'll clean your bike. I'll clean your shoes. Anything you want.'

'Shut up or I'll thump you.'

I shut up.

He gives me a long dangerous scowl that makes me think asking him wasn't such a good idea. Then he kick-starts his bike and cruises down the street, only to chuck a U-ey on the corner and glide back to me.

'Go on then, get on.'

'Yeah? Thanks a lot, Kevin.'

'You can hang on to my waist, but you try stickin' your tongue in my ear and I'll rip it out of yer head.'

'Hang on to your waist? In yer wet dreams. I'd rather fall off.'

BBBRRRUUUUMMMM!

He revs it to about fifty times faster than he's ever done.

Before we reach the end of the street I have his waist in a death lock.

Shakily I climb off the bike outside the Vista.

'How was that?' Kevin flashes a smart-alec grin.

Think fast, Neil.

'Boring,' I say. 'Was the handbrake stuck?'

BBBRRRUUUUMMMM!

I charge up the steps and find Sylvie already there.

17

'Hey, Sylvie. I'm not late, am I?'

'No, you're perfect.'

She gives me the most beautiful smile I've ever seen. I nearly look around to see who's behind me.

'I'm so glad you could make it. Come on.'

I stride ahead to open the glass door for her. It's heavy and I almost can't do it.

Push! Push! But make it look easy!

'Ah. I see you're a gentleman,' she says. 'I like that.'

She walks with me when we go inside; not dashing off in front or hanging back, but beside me and close. It's like she's really my girlfriend.

'There he is.' She points at Zom. 'He hasn't seen us. Let's get in the queue and surprise him.'

My eyes carry out a lightning raid over her boobs – if she caught me perving I'd have to kill myself. I can't really tell much in a raid that lasts a fraction of a second, but I'm guessing they're just right. She could have six of them, all different sizes and colours and glowing in the dark, and I'd still be happy. Her head reaches up to just above my shoulder. It's the ideal height for holding and kissing. I've got no complaints in any area.

'Well, hello there, Mr Usher.' Sylvie grins at Zom. 'I hope you know what you're doing.'

'Nope – haven't got a clue. Hi, Sylvie. Hey, Neil – good to see you.'

We wait until everyone goes inside for the movie and then Zom has a break and sits with us on a black leather sofa in front of the snack bar, the smell of popcorn so strong you could almost choke on it.

He tells Sylvie about his job: 'The only thing I have to remember is, don't let anyone in without a ticket. It's not much of a job.'

'Aw, it's all right,' I say. 'Better than my brother Kevin's first job – he worked down at the greyhound track on Wednesday nights; had to walk behind the dogs as they went to the starting boxes and pick up any poos they did. I loved it when he had that job. I used to call him Poo Man.'

'I suppose this is a bit of an improvement on that,' Zom says.

'Well, I think it's great.' Sylvie pulls on his bow tie before letting it snap back into position. 'And I'm very proud of you.'

I should get her to give Kevin some tips about how to treat a brother.

18

Sylvie pays for my movie ticket. 'I insist,' she tells me. I compromise by telling her I'll buy the ice-creams. Zom says we still have a few minutes before the movie starts – we've only missed the ads and the cartoons – just enough time for Sylvie to duck off to the toilet.

'Looks like things are getting back on track now,' I say once she's gone. 'You've got a job and a place of your own to live. You're a legend.'

He grins and nods. A runaway clump of hair falls over his eyes. If I have wondered about Zom at all since I saw him last, it's only because of one thing . . .

'You ever think of Brother Mick these days?' I say, making it as casual as I can.

'All the time. That won't change. I still don't know what I'm going to do, but the day will come.'

I look at him long and hard, trying to work out where the truth ends and lies begin. I'm a bit of an expert at lies, and I can't see any coming from him.

'Okay, Zom. Just wonderin'.'

I take a deep breath and move on. 'About this movie I'm seeing with Sylvie. Just so you know – it was her idea, since I was here anyway to see you. It's not like a proper date or anything ... actually I'm not really sure what it is.'

'Maybe she likes you, Neil.'

'Nah. No way ... I hardly know her. I don't even know what she does for a job – she said something about shift work.'

'She's a nurse. In the Casualty ward at the hospital.'

'Cool. A nurse, eh. She looks a bit like a nurse.'

'Does she? What do they look like, Neil?'

'Like your sister, dopey.'

His face creases up when he laughs and his eyes just about disappear.

'Hey, Zom, be honest – do you think she might like me?'

'I wouldn't know.'

'Has she said anything to you about me?'

He mulls over the question like it's a problem deep and mysterious that needs to be untangled.

'Zom. I need an answer today. Sylvie's coming back. Quick. Has she talked about me – yes or no?'

'Not really ... except when she screams out your name in the middle of the night.'

'Bull. She does not ...'

I want to hear him say it's really true but instead he laughs. I didn't know Zom could tell jokes.

We go in to watch the movie. Zom said I'd like it. It's called *Here We Go Round the Mulberry Bush*. Sounds pretty lame to me but I soon find out it's okay. It's set in England and there's good music and plenty of funny scenes and it has this hot blonde in it named Judy.

With the light shining off the screen I see Sylvie's face clearly. She's smiling nearly all the way through and laughing. Gleaming white teeth. Her lips are the ideal shape. And they look as soft as marshmallow. I think about sneaking my arm around behind her and casually dropping it onto her shoulders. Just as quickly I dismiss the idea. The closest I've been to a girl is a centrefold and now I'm talking about doing the arm drop manoeuvre.

Don't go there, Neil. It's like playing Russian roulette with all the bullets.

What if she slaps me or screams or just looks at me like I'm a low-life? What if she tells her mad father? There are far too many what-ifs. Forget that. I like living too much. Anyway, I'm happy enough just sitting next to her. On top of that, the movie is getting real interesting. Judy and her boyfriend run down to the river – it looks like something could happen – yep, they start stripping off their gear. I don't get too excited at first because for sure they'll cut to another scene. They always do . . . but not this time. Jeez. Bit by tantalising bit Judy peels off every stitch. Totally nude. I mean, she stands straight in front of the camera and you can take the whole tour. Holy moley. You were right about this movie, Zom. It's Academy Award material.

At that moment something strange happens. Sylvie's leg bumps against mine. One bump I could understand, but it goes on three or four times. I ignore it, of course. I glance at her face and there's no change of expression. She's still watching the movie. Must have been an accident. She'd be embarrassed if I told her so I go on as if nothing happened. A few minutes later, when Judy has her clothes back on and I can prise my eyes from the screen, I take another peek at Sylvie. It's a different face now. Her smile has disappeared. She's frowning. I'm really puzzled.

For some reason Sylvie seems a little cool and remote when it's time to say goodbye. I tell her I had a good night and she says she did, too, but she fires it back like a reflex action, and I don't fully believe it. There's no mention of a next time. A kiss on the cheek is never a possibility. She gives me nothing, not even the offer of a lift.

On the way home I convince myself this is the best thing that could have happened. She's not only too old, she's too moody. I'm glad it wasn't a real date. If it had been, now I'd have the problem of working out how I was going to dump her without hurting her feelings too much.

At three o'clock in the morning I sit up in bed, suddenly wide awake and filled with horror.

What if those bumps to my leg weren't because she's clumsy? What if she was trying to send me a message?

It happened in the middle of a nude scene. That might have been a clue.

Jee-zus.

'Stupid, stupid – I am so STUPID!'

Kevin chucks a pillow at me.

Still half asleep, he garbles, 'Just because you're stupid, doesn't mean I won't kill you.'

19

I wish I had someone to talk with about Sylvie.

Usually I tell all my stuff to Troy, not that there's ever much to tell. This time I can't. He doesn't want to know anything about Zom, and I'm sure the same goes for anyone in his family.

I can't talk to Kevin because, well, for one, he probably wouldn't listen, and for two, if he did listen, he'd laugh. We hardly ever have serious conversations.

Dad would be happy to hear me out and give advice, but I'm too embarrassed to tell him. Same with Mum. The thought of me doing leg-wrestling with a girl at the movies might be a bit of a shock to her– she thinks I'm still her little boy.

I wait a few days, hoping maybe she'll ring, and then I can't wait any longer. I go around to Sylvie's flat.

This time when I stand at the door, I hear voices from inside. Sylvie and a man, not a gawky schoolkid like me, a man. They're only talking. It might be just a cousin or an uncle visiting for a cup of coffee. But then I remember something she said that first day I met her – *I'm not the good Italian girl Dad was hoping for*. All I have to do is knock on the door and I'll know for sure. I do want to know the truth, but not if it's going to hurt.

I walk away, come back, and then once and for all, I walk away.

I spend hours writing letters to her. In most of them I get stuck after 'Dear Sylvie'. I can't mention the leg thing because, what if it really was an accident? And if I take that out I'm not left with much more than the X at the end.

Is it okay to give her an X when I hardly know her?

Is one X a bit miserly?

Are two Xs over-enthusiastic?

What about a whole row of Xs? That's what I'd really like to give her.

Kevin walks past my door and stops to look in. Rose is with him. He's holding her hand; her head is snuggled into his shoulder. Looking at them, I see the truth. If I had any real connection with Sylvie I'd be able to talk to her, hold her. But I can't even write her a letter. I know it then. It's hopeless.

'Who you writing to?' Kevin asks.

I screw up the last piece of paper and throw it into the bin.

'No one,' I tell him.

20

School takes over my life again. This morning we have Brother Hugh for Geography. He's old and fat and sometimes he dozes off – especially if you get him in the afternoon. Hughie's funny – but not on purpose. Instead of saying 'Hang on' or 'Wait a second', he says 'Wait a dick'. I think he means 'tick' but it always comes out as 'dick'. He grunts before he says it, as if he's on the toilet and he's having trouble. Once he was giving John Kellner the strap and the Angelus bells rang, so Hughie says, 'Errggh – wait a dick' and we bow our heads and recite the Angelus, then as soon as it's over he goes back to the strapping. Even Kellner thought that was funny – not immediately, but eventually.

We all pay attention to Hughie, not so much to learn anything, but to hear him say the famous words. He must be in on the joke because not a class goes by without him saying it at least once. When he does, you can hear it whispered all around the room. 'Errggh – wait a dick.'

***

Next up it's Brother Geoffrey. He is tall and skinny under the black robe all the Brothers wear. Not much hair clinging to his long bony head. Still, he parts his hair like the good old days, as if he's trying to tame a forest instead of four or five puny strands.

He calls his strap Louie. Like all the straps the Brothers use on us, it's got strips of lead sewn into the business end. But Geoffrey is all right. He doesn't hit you for the fun of it or lose his temper like some of the others. When he straps you there's always a good reason for it, and it's never personal.

Now he's roaming around the room checking homework. If you didn't do it, it's two cuts, maybe three or four. Depends on your record. Mine's bad. Troy looks at me and knows straight off I didn't do last night's homework. Hardly ever do. I can see from his expression that for once he did his.

I'm part of a group of regulars who just can't get into the homework habit. Troy is usually the same, unless his father stands over him, like he must have done last night. Geoffrey says the reason we don't do homework is because we're lazy. That's partly true, but there are other reasons . . .

Homework is boring.

TV is much more interesting.

We've got too many hormones.

Of these three, hormones are my biggest problem. They're like the devil's soldiers. They won't leave me alone. In the past I've flitted from one fantasy girlfriend to another – a centrefold or a face and body picked out of a crowd. Now I find myself returning to Sylvie, no matter how much I vow to forget her. We have some really good times together. I only wish she knew about it.

'Psst.' Troy catches my attention. 'Here.' He holds out his exercise book for me to take.

'Nuh.' I shake my head. 'But thanks.'

Geoffrey perches on top of one desk after another, leaning forward and back, then swivelling from side to side, inspecting homework all around. Two more to look at before he gets to me. This is an emergency. Time to ask God for help. Is begging a prayer?

Please God, get me out of this. I'll be good if you do. I promise.

Paul Evans is strapped. One of the regulars. He doesn't flinch. Big burly second rower. Bounce him on his head and it wouldn't bother him. No one takes much notice as Louie strikes. It's part of every day, like the bell ringing, like the pissy smell around the toilets.

Troy shows his homework. Geoffrey doesn't care if it's right or wrong, only that it's done. He gives it a tick with a red pen and scribbles his initials. I'm next. He reaches over to pick up my exercise book. I half stand to take my punishment. But then he scratches his ear, runs a finger back and forth under his itchy nose. And lifts himself off the desk and strolls back to the front of the class. Forgetting all about me.

The word gets out about my great escape. It travels fast and by the time we're walking down the corridor I'm getting thumped on the back like I'm a hero. Bails wallops my arm as he passes me and calls me a lucky bastard. Trevor Findlay reckons Brother Geoffrey must be losing his marbles. Troy tells me to live it up while I can – 'Because he'll get you next time.'

Right now it seems like next time is a million light years away and not worth worrying about. I feel like I've won the lottery, and I didn't even buy a ticket. It's one of my very best days.

21

It's the first lesson after lunch. We're waiting for our new teacher but he hasn't arrived yet. We've seen him only once, at Assembly. Didn't give him a second glance. Just another teacher. It's raining heavily outside and hammering on the tin roof. Kind of loosens everything up when the weather's like this. Our school's all straight lines and *do this, do that*. But now in this howling rain no one's watching us. Kids out of their seats, kids shoving each other, throwing stuff. Me and Troy are sitting on top of our desks, talking in whispers about sex as if we're the only ones who know about it. That's all we're doing.

'Quiet!'

The voice thuds into the room first. One step behind is the new teacher.

In seconds everyone is at his own desk. The teacher doesn't need to tell us to sit up straight and pay attention. That was stamped into our brains years before.

He's a lay teacher. We've got three others, Mr Matthews – who only takes us for PE – and Mr Wilson and Mr Harris. All the rest are Brothers. Apart from Johnno every one of them is handy with the strap. Some only use it as a last resort. Some whenever they feel like it. Mick and Clementian are the worst offenders, but that's all right because you know what they're likely to do and that helps you handle it. This new teacher is something else. It's all unknown territory with him. I can feel the danger.

'My name is Mr Delaine. I will be teaching this class Mathematics.'

His hair is black and smooth with oil. His face is cratered by acne. His suit is dark blue, his eyes hidden behind sunglasses so we can't tell who he's staring at.

'Out the front.' He nods at Alan Honan.

Honan stands and stumbles to the front of the class-room. 'Me, sir?'

He's the school captain, always in the top three when we have exams. No one ever gives Honan the strap. He's the golden boy.

'You. Put out your hand.'

'But I didn't do anything.'

'Did I ask you to speak? Hand. Out.'

Three cuts with the strap.

'Other hand.'

'But, sir –'

'You don't want to make me lose my patience, boy. Believe me.'

Honan holds his left hand unsteadily and takes three more.

'Sit down. Now all of you. Out the front. Form two lines. One on each side of me.'

We know better than to argue or ask questions. We go easily, without complaint, maybe because it doesn't seem possible that he'll strap the whole class.

'You first.'

Soon we know how possible it is. He won't listen to questions. He won't take excuses. Six of the best for all of us.

A few pull their hands away. To stop them doing it again they cop one around the legs. It hurts twice as much there. The voice cuts into them as sharp as the strap: 'Put your hand out. Now.'

I don't pray this time. I just know it won't work.

22

A bunch of my classmates cry and they don't care who knows about it. For most, being cool isn't an issue right now. Pain blanks out all that stuff. No one sniggers or looks down on them. We all understand how much it hurts.

Troy is next. He turns back to me, to the class, and winks, a grin smeared across his face. I don't know if the teacher sees it or not but it seems he packs extra power into hitting Troy – maybe he just picks him as one who needs special attention. He whips the strap down harder and faster. After the third one I see Troy's legs shaking. After the fourth Troy holds his hand under his arm trying to find some relief from the pain. He leaves it there too long and the strap lashes the back of his legs. Troy buckles and gasps then sucks in a breath and holds out his hand again, for the fifth, for the sixth.

He walks quickly back to his seat, eyes to the floor, the grin hacked out of him. But then he breaks. His face twists and grimaces, his mouth opens, and he cries. Troy looks away fast when he catches me watching. I wish I hadn't seen him. Neither of us has anywhere to hide.

Now it's my turn. I know the strap is coming but it's still a shock. I'm not conscious of anyone else in the room except the figure in front of me and the strap, flashing down. It's the same each time; a jolt of electricity, raw pain. I can never get used to this, never be prepared for it. My hands feel like they're burning up from the inside. I don't know why I'm not crying too. It's got nothing to do with being brave. I'm barely holding it together, like everyone else. Maybe I'm not smart enough to cry – 'no sense, no feeling,' Clementian says. Or maybe I'm too stubborn.

I've had the strap a heap of times – more than I can remember. Usually for not doing my homework. That's fair enough. Most often it's one or two whacks for little things: being out of uniform, talking in class. And when I've got a six, I've had a good time earning it. We don't hate the Brothers for using the strap. You take it and forget it. But I don't think any of us are going to forget this. He gives the whole class six each on his first day. He doesn't even tell us why.

Now the last boy is back in his seat. The room is absolutely silent. Not even the ones with tears glistening in their eyes dare to sniffle. The teacher stands with his arms at his sides, holding the strap ready to go again as if that first round was just a rehearsal.

'My name is Mr Delaine. I will be teaching this class Mathematics. Are there any questions?'

No one says a word.

For the rest of the day, long after the ache has left our hands, the new teacher invades our thoughts and conversations. We wonder what's up with him; whether he's crazy or just sadistic. A bit of both, most of us decide.

We've got some good teachers.

Mr Wilson has us for English. You have to just about set him on fire to get him stirred. Once he praised a story I wrote. He gave me this big build-up in front of the class. Since then he's always been my favourite teacher.

Last year Brother Geoffrey took us on a bus into town to see *The Sand Pebbles*. He didn't have to do that; even better, he let us talk him out of taking us to watch *The Bible*.

There are others I like, too, but I don't think about them much. They don't dog my footsteps home or crowd my head with thoughts when I try to sleep –

scared and angry thoughts. And of all the bad teachers this one's the worst, the meanest – the new champion of the strap. Delaine.

23

Going home it's all blue sky and sunshine, as though we just dreamed the rain. We spill out onto the footpath of Sandy Bay Road and file down it in a ramshackle stream of ones and twos, threes and fours. I'm a one. Slouching along ahead of me is Troy.

'Hey. Hang on.' I jog over to him. 'What's yer hurry?'

He stops until I catch up but then ploughs on, head down as if he's the only one left in the world. I know he's really down about today. A finger-snap – that's how long anyone will remember that he cried. I could tell him that for a hundred years and he wouldn't believe it. It's bad when you can see someone falling but you can't do a thing to stop it. I feel that way now about Troy. He'll go home and sit in his room, drawing for hours. He draws comic book superheroes and monsters. Tonight I reckon the monsters will look a lot like our new teacher.

I grab his arm. 'Hey, it doesn't matter what happened today.'

He pulls away from me. 'Never said it did, did I?'

'Then get over it. Forget that prick of a teacher. Okay, today was bad, but I'll bet it never happens again.'

'How would you know?'

'I just know. It was a one-off.'

'You don't know anything, Bridges.'

He never calls me by my last name.

'I don't want to be here anymore.' He says it as much to himself as to me. 'It's like this all the time. They win. I've had enough.'

That knocks me sideways. While I try to think of something to say he stomps off, so alone. I call after him. 'Troy. Wait a second.' He keeps going.

I understand how he feels. It's hard enough when you know what to expect from teachers, when you've got them all worked out and labelled. You still can't relax, but you have a rough idea what might happen; you can be ready for it. You can't be anything but scared when a teacher smashes all the rules, first day; just drops on you like a brick, with no reason.

I catch up and walk by Troy's side.

'At the very most it'll be just these first couple of days that might be bad – but today was the worst of it, right? It can't get any worse, can it?'

No answer, but I keep trying.

'Concentrate on the weekend. No school. No stupid teachers. We'll do something – both days if you like. Go fishing or bowling – you can come over to my place and listen to records. I'll even go do that dopey trick with the trains again! Anything you want, I'm up for it. I know – we can catch a train into Sydney – check out The Cross. You've always wanted to do that. Come on, Troy. You with me?'

'I'm not going back to school,' he says. 'Not ever.'

'Now you're talkin' crap. Your parents won't let you leave. Even if they did, who'd give you a job? What would you do? You're hopeless – same as me.'

He walks on as if I'm not there. I make sure he knows I am.

'TROY!'

'What?'

'Listen to me. Today was a stunt. Delaine wanted to get our attention. He was letting us know who was boss, that's all. Now everyone will stay in line and he'll be just another teacher. You'll see. You've just got to hang in there.'

He stops walking. For a few seconds he considers it. His future hovers in the breeze. Stay with the devils you know, or go looking for new ones.

'Hey, I need you here, Troy.' I flick on the crooked

smile that tells him an insult is heading his way. 'Right now I'm only the second most stupid kid in the school – if you go I'll be Number One. You can't do that to me. I don't want your title.'

I think I've hauled him back, only to hear, 'Sorry, Neil. I've made up my mind. You'll be fine. All right?'

'No, it's not all right!'

He wanders off the footpath and stands behind a parked car, looking at me.

'Well . . . it'll have to be. I'll see you around.'

'What? When will I see yer?'

Troy smiles, just faintly. Then he takes a couple of steps backwards onto the road, still half looking at me.

I shrug. 'See yer Monday – you better be there.' I turn and walk away. Then I hear a heavy dull *thwack*. I look back and see what looks like a big box or a bundle of something, hurtling along the centre of the road, scraping over the bitumen for fifty yards until it stops.

I don't understand what's happening. I think to myself, it can't be human, whatever it is. It lies in the centre of the road. Doesn't make a sound. Doesn't move.

Cars pull up. People are running from all directions. Then someone is yelling, 'It's Bosley! It's Bosley! He got hit by a car!'

I make it onto the road. Hiding behind faces in a pack. A space opens up and I see the thing that everyone is staring at. It has to be him. Troy. But the more I stare, the less certain I am. It doesn't look like anything.

24

I'm usually home by four-thirty at the latest. It's after six now and I'm only just walking into my street. I don't remember how I got here or where the time went. I've been wandering, trying to work things out. Stuff has been spinning around in my head non-stop. I know there was an accident and someone was killed. A big part of me says it has to be Troy. But I still don't know for absolute sure. It happened so fast. He was talking to me and then there was a crash and he was gone and then I saw this bloodied torn lump. I got out of there as quick as I could. I should have stayed and looked around for him. Should have asked someone. When I get home there might be a phone message from him. There has to be. It doesn't seem possible that he could be dead.

Mum's waiting near the front gate. She runs up to me with her arms out wide.

'Neil. Thank God.'

That's all she says. Hangs on to me like she's dragged me back from the grave. Dad isn't far behind. Kevin's there too.

'We been out lookin' for yer.' Dad's eyes are steady on me, but it's sadness in them, not anger. 'Never mind,' he tells me, taking a step closer to tap my shoulder. 'Long as you're all right. That's the only thing that matters.'

Kevin and I have always been at war. I've lost count of all the punches I have to pay him back for. Now all that disappears. He stacks a whole lot of feeling into just a squeeze of my arm and a nod. I wish he wasn't being nice to me. It tells me something's very wrong. And Mum underlines it all by crying.

We go inside the house, into the lounge room. I'm sitting in Dad's armchair, which is the one thing he gets stroppy about. *Get your own chair. This one's reserved.* Today it's different. He's told me to sit here. Now he's standing in front of me with his arms folded. Mum and Kevin are silent. They're waiting for Dad to say something but he's having trouble getting started.

I know it can be only one thing. I don't listen when he says it. Don't want to hear. Don't want to believe. I close my eyes tight and concentrate on Troy's face. When he was alive.

25

That night our house is like a library asleep. No TV for the first time that I can remember. No radio. The phone rings once. It smashes the quiet like a sledge-hammer.

When we eat the only conversation comes from Kevin. 'That was Rose before on the phone. Told her I might go over and see her later on. Just catch up. Listen to records. I bought her this new Bob Dylan . . .'

He chews on a piece of meat and waits for some reaction. Dad looks briefly at Mum as if he's passing the baton, letting her decide what to say.

'It would be nice if we could all stay together tonight, Kev.' She reaches across the table and pats his hand. 'I think Rose will understand.'

Kevin nods. 'No dramas, Mum. You're right. I'll give her a call. She'll be sweet. I'll see her tomorrow anyway.'

* * *

The lights are on in just about every room. Mum had it the same way when Gran died. Probably some cavewoman instinct: light a big fire and huddle around it when there are wild beasts nearby. I reckon death is a wild beast . . . I hate it.

Dad suggests we sit at the kitchen table and say a silent prayer for Troy. He usually lets Mum lead the way in the prayer department. Not tonight. We take our places and bow our heads. I try to pray, but I can't do it. You have to concentrate to pray and my mind's a rollercoaster out of control. Reliving what happened – that's the ride I'm on – around and around.

Mum clenches her rosary beads in front of her heart and mouths an endless line of Hail Mary's. Dad lowers his head devoutly but spoils the look by yawning. Most nights he falls asleep in front of the TV. His snowy hair is thin and fading. There's a round spot in the centre that is bald. Dad was forty-one when I was born. He's always been old to me. One prayer that comes easily to me is this: *Please God, let Mum and Dad live another twenty years.* I say that sometimes, not every day because most of the time I think they're never going to die. But I say it tonight. In twenty years I'll be thirtysix. At that age death won't be able to touch me. I'll be able to handle anything that comes along. Right now it's not so easy.

Kevin closes his eyes but I don't think he's doing any praying.

'I've outgrown God.' That's what he told me a year ago when he stopped going to Mass. 'The same's gunna happen to you, Neil. You wait and see.'

I laughed then. Called him a wanker and ran for my life. Didn't give it a lot of thought till now. You grow up a Catholic and you wear it like an old familiar coat. Don't even notice you're putting it on half the time. Some people, like Mum and Dad – especially Mum – they're mad-dog believers. Nothing sways their faith. They live for God. Not my style. I've always been a slacker about religion. I drift along. Do my own thing. But when I'm in trouble it's: 'Hey, God, remember me?' So when it comes to the crunch I suppose I do believe. God watches over us. He loves us. That's what I've been taught since Day One.

But now Troy is dead. I'll never see him again.

I can't stop wondering why God would let it happen.

Later, when Mum and Dad have gone to bed, Kevin calls me into our room. Most times I'd think it was a trap to rumble me. I know that's not the reason now. He puts on his Bob Dylan record. It's turned down so low we can hardly hear it, but I don't care. Sitting on the floor with Kevin, watching the record wobble around, it helps the night go.

26

Dad takes me to the police station the next day.

'Nothing to worry about, Neil,' he says. 'The police have to do their job. It's only natural they want to talk to you, since you were with Troy when it happened. It won't take long.'

We wait at the front desk until the cop handling Troy's case ambles out.

He guides us down a narrow passageway into a poky office bursting with paper and photos and files and brown-stained coffee mugs, and now, us. He nods towards two chairs and shuts the door.

Grimacing, he pulls off his tie and stuffs it in a drawer.

'Now tell me ... Neil ... what happened.'

I give him the few details I know. It isn't much but he writes it down. All the while I stare behind him at the Wanted posters on the wall. I think some part of me is searching for a picture of Delaine.

'Neil?'

Dad's looking at me.

'Yep?'

'Constable Adams asked you a question.'

'Sorry.'

'That's all right, matey.' He hits the smile button. It lasts a second, no more. 'I was wondering about Troy. You knew him well, I take it.'

Dad answers. 'They were really close.'

'It's tough when that happens.' The cop notices some dandruff on his shirt and brushes it away. It crosses my mind that Troy isn't very important to him at all. 'So, Neil, how was your mate yesterday? Anything strange going on with him? What was his mood like?'

I panic and try not to show it. That probably means I show it twice as much. I wasn't expecting this kind of question.

'Normal.' I shrug. 'Same as always.'

I feel Dad's arm around my shoulder, holding me together.

'Neil's doing it hard, Officer.'

'You see, the thing is,' he flips the top of the pen up and down, 'the driver – a lady, it was – she says this young fella, Troy, he just lobs onto the road in front of her. Like, he's not walking across the road, he's not running. None of that. There are no skid marks, so she hasn't put her brakes on. It backs up what she says. One second the road is clear, nothing but daylight, the next – *bang*.'

My mouth is dry. I feel my hands begin to sweat.

'She wasn't speeding. Hadn't had a drink. Perfect driving record. So that's why I was asking about young Troy's mood.'

He pauses, and then looks directly at me.

'You are really the only one who might be able to give us some answers. Can you think of anything at all that might be able to help us? Did he say anything unusual?'

There's a code you don't break. Whatever happened, it stays between me and Troy.

'No . . . nothing.'

At last we're led to the front desk. The cop's tie is back on.

'This job's all about paperwork.' He pushes open the door that leads out onto the street. 'Cross your t's and dot your i's. Bloody routine. Drive a bloke up the wall, it would.'

He shakes Dad's hand. I wipe mine on my pants to get rid of the sweat, but there's no need – he only nods to me.

'A couple of higher-ups still have to sign off on this, but my report will say it's an accident. No one's fault, really. Dreadful business. Anyway, thanks for coming in.'

Going home the words from the police interview keep pounding me.

This young fella just lobs onto the road in front of her – not walking across the road – not running. One second the road is clear, nothing but daylight, the next – bang.

'Neil?'

'Yes, Dad?'

'If there's ever anything you want to talk about – with me or your mum – you know you can, right?'

'Sure.'

I see Troy clearly at that moment before it happened. When he stepped onto the road he was looking at me.

'Good, mate, good. As long as you know we're here for you. Always.'

A handful of seconds go by, a lot of images and thoughts . . .

'Dad?'

He faces me, waiting.

I grope for the words but they're too hard to say. I don't even want to think them.

'It doesn't matter,' I tell him. 'It's nothing.'

.

When it's near dark I go for a run. It can get pitch black and I won't care. I could run these streets in the middle of the night. I did it once with Troy, for a dare. It seemed like every dog in town woke up to bark at us.

There's peace in running. You switch off your brain and concentrate on the next step and nothing else. It's like putting yourself on an island. If you really get into it, you don't hear your shoes hitting the ground; after a while your breath has no sound, or your heart. Sometimes you can just about disappear. The one thing you can't do, though, is outrun a ghost.

27

The funeral is in three days' time. That's too soon, but even if it was a month away I wouldn't be ready for it. Brother Mick decides my class can't attend the service. It's just for the family, he says. I'm too weak to stand up to Mick. Even though I want to be there, and I feel like I should, a part of me doesn't really mind. I don't know if I could handle it.

The senior classes are to form a guard of honour outside the church.

Mick rams home our instructions. 'Every boy must be in his proper uniform. That means a clean school blazer, no matter what the weather is like. I want to see your ties straight and your shoes shined. You will be representing your school. There will be no excuses.'

I hate him standing over us for something like this. 'Just once,' I tell him in my head, 'leave us alone – let us breathe.' It makes me want to turn up in shorts and thongs. Troy would probably think it was a fantastic idea. But Mick wouldn't be too thrilled.

Now it's 10 am. Funeral day. We're lined up in two long rows, one on each side of the church door. You always get some fool sneaking a few whispers and jokes out when the Brothers aren't looking, but it doesn't happen today. We stand there close to an hour, baking under the sun but barely moving. I look down the row and see it straight and solemn. Like we've all grown up in just four days. Then they carry out the box and it's got flowers heaped on it. I see Troy's mum and dad and his two sisters and they're all hanging on to each other, like that's the only way they can stand up. They slide the box into the black car and we watch it drive away. I decide I'm glad we're all polished up and clean. A life has to be worth that much.

That afternoon at home, Mum uses hugs on me like they're bandaids and I'm cut to pieces. Dad isn't into hugging. His way of getting close is playing backyard cricket with me. He does it now and it's not even Sunday. Kevin joins in. There must be something he could be doing with Rose, but he stays with us. They let me hog the bat. Kevin's the wicketkeeper. Dad trundles down his old-bloke spinners, which usually end up as wides.

Mum stays on the verandah. She's the crowd. Her job is to cheer every time I make a run, and hang on to Dusty in case she chases down the ball and eats it.

The cricket is like a small, delicious square of choco-late. In the moment there's nothing better in the wide world. I don't think of anything but the game and the fun. But it's gone too fast. Soon it's night again and I'm in my bed; eyes wide, thoughts tearing me up.

28

First day back at school after the funeral: *awkward* is the only word for it. I get consoling pats on the back and lots of questions, all asked out of duty, trying to do the right thing.

'What's happenin', Neil? You goin' all right?'

I know they're desperate for me to say I'm fine, so that's what I tell them. I'd be the same if I was in their place. Death's too hard for any of us.

Bails walks beside me and for once he spares me his corny stories. He just walks. It's good to have some back-up as I move past the sea of curious faces. School has been my world for so long and yet today I feel like a stranger. Your best mate dying changes things.

We're on our way to Assembly when I hear a cold, familiar voice behind me.

'Leave us for a moment,' he tells Bails.

And then I'm alone with Delaine.

It's ten to nine in the morning on an overcast day, but he's still wearing his sunglasses. Behind the glasses I make out black pits; two crocodile eyes, just below the water, waiting . . .

'Son.'

I hate him calling me that.

'I want you to know that I'm sorry about your friend. It was a tragic thing.'

He stops. That's it. He's run out of nice things to say. Now he's waiting for me to say something back. I'm too stunned to answer; amazed that he's talking to me – amazed that he thinks I'd talk to him.

He stares at me and I hold my breath, the way you would if someone had a gun to your head.

At last I hear: 'Go on now. Don't be late for Assembly.'

As I walk away I sift through Delaine's words, his tone, trying to find the sarcasm, the menace. There isn't any. I'm surprised and, in a way, disappointed. Anger has been festering in me. I need someone to blame. I'll never know for sure what happened on the road that day, but I know it was Delaine who was on Troy's mind in the moments before he was killed. I keep thinking that if he hadn't come to our school and gone on the rampage the way he did, Troy would still be alive.

But then, he didn't have to say he was sorry about

Troy. And he wouldn't have said it unless he meant it. I look back at him and see just another teacher. He didn't push Troy under that car. It isn't his fault.

It's hard to let go of the anger. It's all I have.

Still, I force myself to walk back and stand in front of him.

'Thanks, sir.' He stares at me. 'For saying that about Troy. It means a lot.'

He replies with a microscopic nod and one gruffly spoken word: 'Assembly.'

29

In the early days after the funeral the teachers hit me with the Invisible Ray instead of the strap. They know I was closest to Troy, so maybe they think I've caught enough hell for a while. They don't see me when the hard questions are being asked or the punishments are being meted out. I expect Delaine to be the exception, but he leaves me alone too. It feels as if I've been given a free pass from real life.

Troy's desk remains empty for a day, and then a new kid moves in and treats it like he's the only one who's ever sat there. He must wonder why I stare at him sometimes.

At home, my parents excuse my rotten temper and surly grunts as all part of the grieving process. When I get away with it, it only makes me angrier. I can't explain why.

Even Kevin steps around me instead of stomping all over me like he usually does. One time, when I'm sure he's watching, I twist the mirrors on his bike – I'd break them off if I could. Any other day he'd pummel me, now he just shakes his head, sets the mirrors back where they were, and strolls off.

The anger I've been feeling over so many things explodes.

I go after him, jump onto his back, hit him everywhere I can.

He didn't do anything; his only crime is that he's closest.

At that moment Kevin is Delaine. He's Death. He's God. And he's Troy – Troy who ran out on me.

I hate him.

In an instant my head is trapped inside his arms and all his weight bears down on me. He grinds my mouth into the grass and I taste dirt.

'What is your problem, Neil? You want to die? I can arrange that for you. Just say the word.'

Maybe that is my problem.

'Do it!' I yell back. 'Go on, do it! You gutless wonder! Do it!'

He lets me free. I jump to my feet, ready to go on with it. He stays down.

From nowhere he says, 'My number's come up for Vietnam.'

All of a sudden I don't want to fight him anymore.

'Mum and Dad don't know yet. Only found out today. I'm telling you first. Even before Rose. You know why?'

'No.'

'Well, here it is – take it or leave it. I'm pissed off at your mate Troy.'

'What? He's dead – and you didn't even know him.'

'Yeah. But I know how you feel about him. You're in a bad way. But if I was dead you'd say good riddance.'

'No I wouldn't. I wouldn't.'

'Well, you should. I've never been your friend.'

'Sometimes you have.'

'Not enough. Anyway, I'm going off to Vietnam and blokes get killed over there. I wanted to give you something special before I went so that's why you got told first. You can be a pain in the arse sometimes, Neil, fair dinkum – but I wouldn't swap yer. I want you to know that. You're my brother. And that's okay with me. All right?'

'Yeah, Kev . . . it's okay with me, too.'

'And look, if I do get killed, you can have my bike.'

'Don't say that stuff.'

'It could happen, Neil.'

'Well, if it does, I don't want your stupid bike. You can shove it!'

'It's not stupid. You are. And you're havin' it whether you like it or not. So shove it yerself!'

'That's so typical, Kevin, even when you're dead you'll be bossing me around.'

'You better believe it – loser.' Grinning, he presses his fist to my nose. 'You're never going to get away from me, Neil. Get used to it.'

It's exactly what I needed to hear.

30

Another morning. Another Assembly.

'Mr Bridges! You are chewing gum!'

Clementian swoops down on me like a killer crow.

'Get rid of that disgusting thing, right now. You know the rules.'

'Sorry, Bra.'

'Yes, you'll be sorry, all right. See me in my classroom after Assembly.'

I wait outside Clementian's door. Four others are lined up behind me. He marches briskly up to us as if he can't wait to use the strap. At least we can always count on Clementian to get it over with quickly.

'Inside. All of you.'

I step up first. Only two cuts. It stings like crazy but I've had worse.

Afterwards we gather briefly in a circle outside; spitting on our hands, locking them together and blowing in air to cool them – the usual things you do when it feels like your hands are on fire. Then someone shrugs it off by saying, 'Didn't hurt', and that makes it compulsory for all of us to say the same. As we saunter off to our classes I pass around the chewie.

I guess Clementian hitting me means the Invisible Ray has been lifted. I'm fair game again. That's cool with me. I want to be like everyone else, whether it means getting the strap or not. I'm ready.

31

On Saturday morning I'm on my bed bopping along with Janis Joplin. She's sex on vinyl; frenzied and passionate.

The sound's up high. Rocking the house. It's the only way to listen to Janis.

'Neil.' Mum pounds on the door. 'Neil.'

Later, Janis. I switch her off and open the door.

'Yeah, I know, Mum. Turn down the music. Okay. Already have.'

'That's a very good idea, but it's not about that – yet. There's a young lady to see you. Do you know someone called Sylvie?'

'Yeah. Sort of.'

'Well, don't keep her waiting. She's in the lounge room.'

'Now?'

'Yes. Now.'

'Jeez. Can you stall her, Mum?'

'What on earth for?'

'I think I need to have a shower. I'll be real quick.'

'Goodness me. You'll do, Neil. Just get out there. Go on. Shoo.'

'Hi.' Her face lights up. 'I hope you don't mind me calling in like this.'

'Nah, that's okay.'

I shrug – trying to give the impression I have beautiful women dropping by all the time. I do, too, but not when I'm awake.

'You told me to look you up if I was ever in the area – so I did.'

'Great. It's good to see you, Sylvie.'

'You too. Ray's out in the car. I'm giving him a driving lesson. He's determined to get his licence. I was wondering if you felt like coming for a drive with us. It would give you and him a chance to catch up. What do you think?'

It's a really tough decision.

'Hey, Neil.'

'G'day, Zom. You reckon it's safe for me to be in the car when you're driving?'

'No,' he says.

Sylvie arches an eyebrow. 'Just curious, Neil. Why did you call Ray, Zom?'

I wish I had a rock to burrow under.

'No reason. Just a nickname,' I say. 'I can't even remember what it stands for now.'

Zom decides to be helpful.

'It stands for Zombie,' he says. 'I don't mind it. If you get a nickname it means at least you're not totally ignored.'

Sylvie gives me a long hard stare. I think how good it would be to have her on my side in a debate. She wouldn't need to speak. One look from her is like a blast from a flamethrower.

We cruise around the quiet back streets as Zom has his lesson.

He does a reverse park – almost crashes on the third try. After that I can't bear to look. He does a hill-start and stalls it. We nearly roll back into another car. He's dangerous.

At last we turn onto the expressway.

'I'm better at going straight,' he says, grinning.

'Thank God for that,' I tell him.

Sylvie leans her head back. The breeze throws her hair around and she looks like one of those girls in the shampoo commercials. I could watch her all day.

Zom looks at me in the rear-vision mirror.

'I heard about Troy. That was really bad. I'm sorry, Neil.'

Sylvie swivels around. She says sorry too, without speaking. Like so much with her, it's in her eyes.

We drive on, mainly talking about school.

Zom asks about some of our classmates, some teachers.

'They're all the same,' I say.

'And Brother Michael?'

'Yeah, he's still there. Worse luck. No one's killed him yet.'

Zom doesn't respond.

I decide to stir him a bit: 'I don't think anyone ever will.'

He nods, that's all.

A little further on Sylvie gently punches him on the arm.

'Hey, you,' she says. 'Isn't it about time you told Neil your big news?'

'Aw yeah – I suppose.'

She turns to me. 'It's the best thing that's ever happened to him and he's so casual about it – *"I suppose"* – tell him, Ray.'

'Okay. I've got a new job.'

'What doing?'

'The editor at the *Leader*'s taken me on as a photography cadet.'

'Good one.'

'Isn't that great?' Sylvie smiles at me. 'It's awfully hard to get a cadetship, but Ray's so keen – he's always loved photography.'

'Yes, it's really top stuff,' I say. 'I'm impressed.'

'Thanks, Neil. It's a good place to work and I'm learning heaps . . . it's almost everything I could want.'

'Almost?'

'Well, it would be good if I could share it with my father.'

'He's still not talking to you?'

'No. I don't exist to him.'

Sylvie uses a thumb to wipe the corners of her eyes. She catches me looking.

'A bit of dust,' she says.

After a few moments of silence, she twists around and leans over the back seat.

'Hey, Neil,' there's brightness in her voice now, 'Ray's brought some of his photos to show you. They're in that folio beside you. Take a look. I think he has a lot of potential.'

I flick through photos of sunsets and clouds and

trees, all in grainy black and white. And then I turn a page and see the Brothers' house, taken from several angles. In each photo is Brother Mick – wheeling out the bin, looking in the letterbox, reading a paper on the back porch – every photo unposed, the photographer unseen.

I close the book. In the mirror, Zom watches me.

32

We turn off the main road.

'I thought we'd head for the dam,' Sylvie says. 'Be good to cool off on such a hot day. It's not far now.'

Zom follows her directions and the car winds into the bush, traffic noise fading behind us. We stop in a clearing when the road won't let us go any further.

Sylvie takes her swimming costume from the boot.

'Down this track,' she says. 'The dam's at the end of it. Keep an eye out for snakes.'

The snakes don't bother me as much as Zom. Those photos. That look he gave me . . .

Sylvie ducks behind some trees to get changed.

'We've got to talk,' I mutter to Zom. 'What's with all the pictures of Mick? How'd you get so close anyway?'

'That big tree in the paddock behind their place – climbed it.'

'You're freaking me out.'

'I took some photos, that's all. There's no law against it.'

'They just weren't *any* photos. Why would you do that?'

'I needed to do some research.'

'By climbing a tree?'

'I wanted to see if there was a pattern that I could use . . . something that I could be sure he would do every day. If I can find that out I'll know how I'm going to do it.'

'Mate, you've got to stop. Now I've seen those photos you've made me a part of it – I can't let you do anything to Mick.'

'You've always known, Neil. I told you right from the start. I confided in only you. I trusted you.'

'Zom, Zom . . .'

I run out of words.

'Come on,' he says, 'forget it. I shouldn't have let you see the photos. I won't ever mention it again.'

'But you're still going to do something to him, aren't you?'

'Put it this way, Neil. Every night I pray that God will tell me what to do. Nothing changes.'

'Hey, you two.'

Sylvie steps out of the bushes.

'Are you going to join me?'

She struts to the dam's edge. Her one-piece black costume fits her like a second layer of skin. I marvel at her delicate bumps, and then as she walks past, I marvel again at the secret pink-white flesh on her thigh, revealed as the costume cuts away.

Sylvie's body warms me even more than the weather. Water splashes around me when she dives in, cooling me – at least on the outside.

Zom strips to his underpants.

'You coming in, Neil?'

'I don't think so – we haven't finished talking yet.'

'Maybe *you* haven't, but I have.'

He crashes in.

Sylvie calls out, 'The water's beautiful. You should try it.'

'I'm okay. Maybe later.'

It's good to see her so happy – playing like a little kid, splashing Zom, him splashing her back. I hardly ever see Zom laughing; he is now. It's like there's two of him sometimes. He's just this simple bloke, plodding along, not capable of hurting anyone. Good old Zom. But then there's the other side that only I know . . .

A spray lands at my feet. Then another splats me in the face.

'Oops!' Sylvie grins.

My body wasn't made for swimming costumes. I'm way too skinny. That's why I never learnt how to swim – but the dam is so tempting. Sylvie looks like she's standing up in the water. Zom's beside her. It can't be very deep.

'You don't know what you're missing,' she says. 'You sure you won't come in? It's so refreshing.'

'All right. What the hell – just for a few minutes.'

I kick off my shoes and socks, pants next. I'm in my baggy daggy underpants – never expected anyone would see them. If I have a hormone surge now, with Sylvie watching, I'm going to die. I sit on a rock ledge with my legs crossed so any sudden surge won't be so notice-able – or laughable. Now my shirt comes off. I leave my singlet to the very last second so that my pale and puny chest isn't on display for long, and then I pull the singlet over my head and throw it behind me as I jump.

33

The chill cuts right to my heart. It shocks me awake – more than I've ever been before. I strike out towards Sylvie. I copy the way I've seen it done on TV. Swimming is easy. I stretch out my body and slice through the water. She's in front of me, her arms waiting.

'See? It's good, isn't it?' she says.

Sylvie is so close. I stop swimming to walk the last few steps, and that's when the dam swallows me.

I plunge down.

Panic. Panic.

Thrashing madly. Nothing to hold onto.

The water is brown and dark. I make out Sylvie's legs. Can't reach them.

I bob to the surface, desperately gulping air. She's staring at me. Frozen. Her lips move but I can't hear anything.

I sink again. It's like those nightmares when you're endlessly falling. I'm flailing my arms about as I go down. At last my feet touch the bottom and I kick up, kick up. The water swirls violently with mud.

Once more I make it to the top. Can't see Sylvie. Zom is lying on a rock sunbaking; he has his back to me. My eyes sweep around, at the bushland, the rock bank, the sky.

Quiet and peaceful. Suddenly that's the feeling that sweeps through me.

Dying doesn't scare me now.

I drop down, willing myself to let go this time. I want it.

She grabs me.

Sylvie.

Her hands are dragging and tearing at me, pushing me up. I feel like I'm only half in this world and then my head breaks clear of the water. But Sylvie's gone. I feel her below me, clinging on to my waist, my legs – slipping away. As I drop down again I see her; hair cascading out, arms rising above her head. We're both drowning.

I lunge and grab hold of her. For the first time in my life I don't care about myself. I try to save Sylvie.

And then I'm on my knees and coughing. Whole buckets of the dam spurt out of me. Zom pounds my back. Sylvie stands over me, her arms like a straitjacket around her. She can't stop shaking.

'It's okay now.' Zom remains calm. 'It's over.'

Sylvie's driving. I'm in the back seat with Zom, wide awake and sitting up, but my thoughts are fuzzy. I don't know how I got out of the dam. Don't remember getting in the car. Later on I know I'll feel embarrassed and stupid but right now I'm beyond that. I feel hollowed out, as if part of me is lying at the bottom of the dam.

I don't know how many times I say that I'm sorry, but it doesn't seem enough.

We go to a Chinese restaurant for lunch. Sylvie grins when she sees the name on the menu. The place is called Good Luck.

She reaches across the table and touches my hand, only for a second, but enough. 'That was too close,' she says. 'I never want to do that again. Ray got us both out. Did you know that?'

No, I didn't.

I thank him but he brushes it aside like a speck of dust on his sleeve.

'It wasn't all that close.' He browses through the menu. 'I didn't notice what was happening at first, but when I did,' he shrugs, 'there was no chance I was going to let anyone drown. It just wasn't on.'

During lunch I find out that he and Sylvie were treading water, not standing as I thought. Any fool should have known that, but this fool didn't. After that we don't talk about what happened, but I know that for a long time I won't be able to think of anything else. I should have died today, at sixteen. I almost took Sylvie with me. Zom saved us. Zom, short for Zombie; the hero, the kid who wants to kill a Brother.

Now, more than ever, I don't know what to do about him.

As Sylvie drives me home I think back on the day. It hasn't been a great success. Apart from the drowning episode, now Sylvie knows what I look like in my undies. That's got to put her right off me. Or maybe she's one of those weird people who like blokes who are skinny and dumb – there has to be someone in the world like that. I only wish I knew for sure how she feels. Sometimes I think I've got a chance with her; it's in a look she gives me or the briefest touch of my hand. Every time she pulls back straightaway as if she's afraid of getting too close. I'm afraid of that too, but it might already be too late.

'Take care,' she says as I step out of the car.

I don't tell anyone at home how I nearly drowned. Mum would cry and that would upset Dad. And Kevin would remind me for the rest of my life what a moron I was to jump into a dam when I couldn't swim.

It's okay. I'm full of secrets. One more won't hurt.

34

Back at school again, Delaine sits on the edge of his desk, asking questions about algebra. I tune out because he's working on the other side of the room, taking one desk at a time. With two at a desk it'll be ages before he gets to me. I'll make sure to listen well before that happens. But now is *my* time.

My mind wanders to Sylvie. I play this game where I examine everything she says, searching for a sign that she likes me as more than just a friend. I find plenty of things, but there's never enough to overcome the obstacles. Sometimes I feel so close to her, but I know I can never hold her or kiss her. I can't forget her either. I'm just stuck. Limbo – that's where I am. I write her name again and again in my exercise book, making the letters huge and fancy, shadowing all around them. *SYLVIE*. *SYLVIE*. Maybe this is what being in –

'Bridges.'

Shit.

'Out the front, son.'

I feel the blood draining out of my legs.

'We have been discussing a problem in algebra. Have you been paying attention?'

His eyes burrow into me. The whole class could leave and he wouldn't care. He's got me.

'Yes, sir.'

I don't remember a single word he's said, and he knows it.

He scrawls the problem on the board. I'm bad at algebra at any time but now it's hieroglyphics to me.

'Read it. Think about it.'

'Yes, sir.'

'You can have a minute. Then give me the answer.' I try hard. Re-read every word. Numbers and letters are swirling in circles. Fear won't let me think.

'Hand. Out.'

He only hits me once. Fantastic. I head towards my seat.

'Back up. You are not going anywhere. Look at the problem, Bridges. Give me the answer.'

'I don't know it, sir.'

He turns to the class. 'Who knows the answer?'

Hands fly up everywhere.

'Do you see, Bridges? They know, so it mustn't be too hard. Try again.'

I stare blankly at the board. If I just keep staring maybe the bell will ring and save me.

'Hand. Out.'

He keeps asking the same question. After a while he gives me clues to make it easier. They don't mean anything to me.

'Hand. Out.'

Those are the only words that matter. The question and the clues slip by me because all I can think about is the strap that's coming.

A few kids laugh when I still get it wrong because the answer must be so obvious. There isn't room in my head to be angry with them. I'm just filled up with fear.

'Look at the board, Bridges. Use your brain. Work it out. What does y equal?'

I take a guess – 20, 10. I say anything just to have a chance. Each time he hits me.

The classroom door is open. I seriously think about running away. Right now. I can do it . . . all I need is the nerve.

'Hand. Out.'

It goes on and on and then somehow, long after I thought my brain had shut down, I understand what's happening. If he wanted to hurt me he'd be hitting me more than once each time. And he doesn't really want the answer to the algebra question – because he must know I can't give it to him.

I decide the only reason he keeps me up here is so he can break me.

'You are not trying, Bridges. Give me an answer.'

Now I have a target to aim for – I have to beat him.

For forty-five minutes I stand there. He hits me over and over. Every time it stings and throbs but I refuse to show it. He's not getting anything out of me.

At the end, when the bell rings, when everyone else trundles out of the room, I stand there in front of him. I wish I could say my eyes are cutting into him and I've got him worried. I can't, though. I'm too messed up for anything like that. But I don't run away.

'Go to your next class, son.'

He watches me as I leave the room. I feel his stare hot on my back. I can't imagine Delaine would ever laugh, but if he did, this is the kind of thing that he'd find funny. Maybe he's laughing right now. It's this thought that makes me stop at the doorway.

I turn and face him. 'Sir?'

He doesn't answer, but he's listening.

Say it, say it – no matter what it costs.

'I'm not your son. All right?'

'Over here, Bridges.'

I go to him.

He sits at his desk, arms folded, staring at me. 'Do you have any other clever remarks you'd like to make?'

My turn not to answer him.

He takes off his sunglasses and his eyes are just as dark.

'I don't want to keep your next teacher waiting. That would be rude. So you may go.'

For one breath the world is wonderful ... but only one.

'We'll finish this tomorrow. I want you to think about that tonight. Think about tomorrow, son.'

35

Bails comes up to me after class.

'Jeez, Neil, you really copped it.'

'A bit, yeah.'

'Show me yer hands.'

They're red and swollen. More than they've ever been before.

'I've heard,' he says, rubbing his chin, 'that if yer piss on yer hands it'll stop them from hurting.'

I don't even have to think about it.

'Nah,' I say. 'I'd rather piss on Delaine.'

It's easy to sound tough around my mates, not so easy when I'm back at home with lots of time to think about what's going to happen. Tomorrow he'll be waiting for me. All night long, I can't escape Delaine.

By the time I stagger out of bed Dad's already at work and Mum's been up forever. I mumble to her as we pass and she stops and glares at me until I get the message and kiss her cheek. I shuffle on to the toilet, hop from one foot to the other as I wait, outside the door – *Hurry up! I'm bustin'!* – while Kevin combs his hair real slow. I say a silent prayer for him to go bald.

Mum finally leaves for work, and then Kevin – a piece of toast jammed into his mouth – heads out the door and fires up his bike.

I've finally got the house all to myself. There's plenty of time before I have to catch my bus. I open the front door and take a step outside. It's stinking hot. Already my shirt is clinging to my back. It's going to be a long and sweaty day, but Delaine will be looking forward to it. I wish now that I hadn't back-chatted him. I don't feel so tough anymore.

He's going to get me, unless . . .

Back inside, I lock the door. I can't face today.

I walk around the house closing the blinds at every window so no one can see inside. Through the laundry curtains I look out on to the backyard. Dusty is crouched down on the lawn. Hind legs tucked in under her, front legs hidden beneath her head and chest. She could be a legless dog. Now she stands and stretches. A minute passes before I hear the familiar *patter, patter,* as she climbs the steps onto the verandah. I rap on the window and she looks up at me.

'You can't come in.' I shoo her away with my hands. 'Beat it. Go and chase a lizard.'

She sniffs at the door and whimpers. I walk out there and bang on the door.

'No! Go away!'

A white paw pushes part-way through to me under the door. I touch her furry toe. I'm done for then. Have to open the door.

'Get in here – nuisance.'

Still in my school uniform, I go back to bed. If anyone catches me I'll say I felt sick. But no one's going to catch me.

Dusty sits on the floor, staring at me. Ever hopeful. She's not allowed in the house – except maybe on Christmas Day or if there's an earthquake. But she is never, ever – even during earthquakes – allowed on my bed.

But maybe this is a day for breaking rules . . .

'Come on, girl. Up you get.'

I only have to say it once and she's beside me – happiest mutt in the world. She wags her tail and dog hair flutters everywhere. I'll worry about that later. For now I just want to curl up and be invisible. It's safe here. No one can hit me.

36

I drift in and out of sleep. One time I'm talking to Troy. We're happy and laughing. I almost think it's really happening – don't want it to stop . . . I wish someone would go to the toilet for me. When I finally get out of bed Dusty doesn't stir. She lies on her side, paws twitching in a dream. Now and then she squeaks a tiny, frightened bark, probably fending off a cat that's chasing her. I come to the rescue and wake her. It's nearly ten.

I'm eating the lunch Mum packed for me when the phone rings. I run to answer it but before I get there I know I can't pick it up. There's no one home at our place.

I never knew how lonely our house was. Never knew how slow the day could be if you sat and watched each minute tick past. I flick through comics, spin a record or two, and give up after ten pages of *Huckleberry Finn*. Soon I'm so bored I risk going out into the backyard to throw the ball for Dusty. I keep stepping around the bricks scattered in a messy heap from where Dad knocked down the old barbecue. He hasn't had time to clean them up, but I've got time . . .

It only takes an hour. Every brick squared away nice and neat is a small act of penance to help make up for all my lies. Seems like it's a better idea than praying for forgiveness – I don't think God wants to hear from me.

I'm rubbing Dusty's belly when someone calls out to me, from inside the house.

'Oy! What are you doin' home on a school day?'

Dad.

'Appendicitis.' It comes to me quick as a flash. I hold a hand over my stomach and grimace as I walk towards him. 'I was all ready to go to school and then I got this sudden pain and I just couldn't go.'

'That's no good, matey.' He holds the back door open for me. 'You want me to get a doctor to take a look at you?'

'No, I'll be right, Dad. It's a lot better.'

'Is it now? . . . Hey, Neil – man-to-man –' He drapes an arm over my shoulder and gives me that searching look all parents are expert at. 'Did you really feel crook – or did you just decide to have a day off?'

I dig myself even deeper.

'No, I was sick, Dad. Honest.'

'Fair enough then. You sure you're okay now?'

'Yep.'

'All righty. I'm makin' a pot of tea.' He walks into the kitchen. 'You want a chocolate milk? We've got some ice cubes in the fridge. Seein' yer on the sick list I better look after yer.'

'Thanks.'

'Comin' right up.' A tap runs as he fills the kettle. 'We had a stop-work meetin' today. The Union's tryin' to get us a pay rise.'

While he's talking I scout around the house, getting rid of evidence that says I've been home all day; putting away Huck Finn and the comics I've been reading –

'Think you'll get the rise, Dad?'

– picking up the chips I dropped on the lounge while I watched TV –

'No, they won't have any luck. Not this time. But at least we got off work early, so it's not all bad news.'

– a biscuit wrapper here, a record lying on the floor –

The back door opens. He's emptying the teapot.

'I can't remember the last time I was home this early. It's a beautiful day. Look at that, will you. Not a cloud in the –'

He comes back into the house.

'Those bricks, Neil. You wouldn't know anything about how they got all stacked up like that, would you?'

'Yeah, Dad. I did it. Thought I'd help you out.'

'Today? You did that today?'

Now I really do feel sick.

'Um, yeah.'

'What about your appendicitis?'

I guess my face answers the question for him.

37

Dad takes a seat at the kitchen table. He points to a chair opposite him and I sit down. Head slightly bowed, he folds an arm across his chest and a hand covers his eyes. I know it has to be unintentional, but still, it's the position a priest takes when he's hearing confession. He doesn't say anything straight away and that makes it harder for me. There's nothing as strong as silence.

'I wasn't sick. I just didn't want to go to school.' I blurt it out. 'I'm sorry, Dad.'

'I see.' One hand rakes slowly through his hair. 'Well, I'm disappointed, matey. Not so much that you ditched school – we can work that out. It's that you lied to me when I asked you about it. It's hard to trust someone when they start lying to you.'

School is good in a way because when you do something wrong, it's automatic – you get hit. After that it's not about what *you* did, it's about what *they* did to you.

But Dad doesn't hit me. He just stares at me like he's seeing me for the first time and he's wondering who I am.

He makes his tea and pours it steaming into a cup. I'm looking at the floor when he comes over. As I lift my head he sets a glass of iced chocolate down in front of me. That makes me feel even worse. I don't deserve kindness, but Dad gives it anyway.

'Now I want to know,' he says, 'why would you want to stay home from school?'

No one tells their parents about being strapped. Kevin was the same. He went to my school. You get questions at home, you put up the stone wall. Every single bloke I know feels the same way. You cop the strap and you deal with it yourself – any way you can.

'I hadn't done my homework. I would have been in trouble, so I jigged it. I'm sorry.'

'Are you sure that was the only reason? You weren't being bullied – nothing like that?'

I shake my head. 'There's nothing else to tell.'

It's still only 11.30. 'Plenty of school time left,' Dad says. 'You have to face up to your problems, Neil. They just get bigger if you don't. It might not be as bad as you think it's going to be.'

He wouldn't say that if he knew Delaine.

Dad writes me a 'please excuse' note to explain being late, and then we walk together to the bus stop.

'Do you have to tell Mum about this. 'I ask?

'Jeez. You're asking somethin' there. Your mother and I, we don't have secrets.'

The bus turns the corner at the top of the street.

'I'd like to help you, but the old girl wouldn't be too happy if she found out.'

'I won't tell her, Dad.'

He grins. 'Well in that case . . . you only had a couple of hours off. It's not like you're the Great Train Robber, and you stacked all those bricks for me – despite your burst appendix.'

He smirks and I cringe.

'All right, just this once – we'll keep it between ourselves. But next time, do your homework.'

The bus pulls up in front of us.

'Thanks, Dad.'

38

First lesson after lunch. Delaine.

When I walk into the class I see that the same algebra problem is still written up on the board. He hasn't forgotten about me.

'Bridges. Out the front.'

I glance around the room silently begging for help. No one moves a muscle. I'm alone.

'I've been thinking about you,' he says. 'What to do with you.'

He pauses to glare. If it's supposed to frighten me, it's a good plan.

'You're lazy and you're a time-waster. I've decided I'm not going to bother with you. If you don't want to learn, son, it's your loss. But understand this – when you are in my class you keep your mouth shut and you stay out of my way. Are we clear on that, Bridges?

'Yes, sir.'

'Get a duster.' He points to the board. 'Clean that off. That was yesterday's problem – just like you.'

Cleaning that board is one of the best jobs I've ever been given in school. Every number and letter that vanishes sets me free.

Back at my desk. I keep my head down so he doesn't see my gold-medal grin – but I'm glowing. Yesterday I took on Delaine and today he's got nothing left to throw at me. I beat the mongrel.

But as the lesson draws on I watch him playing his game just as hard and deadly as ever – 'Out the front, son' – and I realise that I haven't beaten him at all, he's just discarded me and moved on to someone else. I'm not important to him. Neither was Troy.

Now I know how Zom must feel about Mick. I'm sure I would never actually do the deed, but I could waste a lot of time thinking about killing Delaine.

But I'm not going to dwell on it.

I won't give him any more power. I don't want Delaine in my head for even a minute. Cut him off. Let him go. Stuff him. I won't kill him. But if he was on fire and a prayer would put him out, I'd forget how to pray.

There are only a handful of weeks to go before the School Certificate and then it's the holidays and the year is over. School is going to be a lot more tolerable without Delaine breathing down my neck, but I don't know why I should tolerate it at all.

Mum has got her heart set on me discovering a cure for cancer, and if not that, at least finding a job where I wear a shirt and tie. I'm her great hope: the first one in the family who won't go home with dirt ground into his fingernails.

That's not me.

'I don't want to go back to school next year,' I tell her.

We're at the kitchen sink peeling potatoes together. We both stop. Mum never raises her voice to win an argument. She always stays calm and collected, even when someone might have put a dent in her heart.

'That's a very big step, Neil. It's not something to rush into.'

'I'm not. I've thought about it a lot. It's what I really want.'

'But why? Help me understand.'

She hears me out as I skate around the edges of the truth, not giving away much but throwing in some hints . . .

'I don't feel very happy at school . . .'

'Sometimes it's not a real good place to be . . .'

'What sort of job would you do?'

'I'll find something. I don't care what it is.'

'But I care, Neil.'

'The School Certificate's coming up. I'm going to study like crazy. Big finish, Mum. I'll get good marks and then I'll be able to score a top job. I'm not the only one in my class who's going to leave. Just say it's all right, Mum.'

'Let me talk it over with your father. We'll see what we can do.'

I know Mum back and front. That's a yes.

39

Tonight at six, Kevin has his medical for the Army. He's always been fearless – any kind of sport, any kind of dare. But I've seen him gradually change since his number came up. When he reads the paper he goes straight to the stories about Vietnam. He watches the war on the TV news. Never says anything about what he reads and sees, just sucks it all in with a bitter look, like he's chucking down poison.

Two hours before the medical I find him in the garage. He's polishing the chrome on his bike; so shiny he can see his face in it. If I had his face I'd be investing in a paper bag to put over my head.

'Mind if I stay out here for a while?' I ask.

'Free country.'

Crouching down beside the bike, I watch him for a while. In my head I'm trying to work out how to ask a tough question in an easy way. Finally I just ask it.

'You scared, Kevin? About Vietnam?'

'Nah. Not really . . .'

He stops cleaning and looks up at me.

'Well, I wasn't before, when it was months away. Now it's happening so fast . . . I've got a mate only a year older than me. He just got shipped back; met him for lunch this week. He had a leg blown off by a land mine. There's worse than that, too. I'll be right, but I think about Rose, you know?'

He closes his eyes and exhales slowly, like he's chasing out all the fear.

'Anyway, like I said, I'll be right.'

'Only the good die young,' I remind him.

'That's right. I got no worries.'

40

At five Rose sets off with Kevin for the test while Mum and Dad wait with me at home.

Right on six o'clock, Mum starts praying.

'Dear God, I'll do any penance, make any sacrifice you ask –'

She sits head down at the kitchen table, just her and the rosary beads. Dad is off having a shower. I'm in my room pretending to do my homework.

'– but please don't take Kevin for Vietnam. He's just a boy. I couldn't bear to lose him.'

I come out when she's finished.

'Don't worry, Mum. Kevin might get through the physical but he'll crash out in the mental part. I don't think the Army takes nut cases.'

'Come here, you.'

She hugs me as if I'm her baby. I don't really mind.

Mum and Dad are on their third cup of tea when at 8.30 Kevin and Rose stroll in.

'Well?' Mum clutches Dad's hand. 'Are you going to tell us what happened?'

'There's not a lot to tell. I got in. Knew I would. Looks like I might be going off to Vietnam to win the war.'

Dad says, 'Well done, mate.'

I put in my little bit: 'Jeez, they must be real hard-up to take you.'

Mum's voice is trembly. 'That's good, sweetie. As long as you're happy.'

Rose puts an arm around her. 'Kevin will be all right, Mrs Bridges. And when he comes home again I'll be waiting for him. I'll look after him for you. Always.'

The room is already quiet before Rose says this, but it becomes quieter still. Mum senses something's going on. Her eyes dart between Rose and Kevin.

'Always?' she says to Rose. 'That's a very strong word.'

'I mean it, Mrs Bridges.'

Kevin moves closer to Rose.

'Mum, Dad – Neil – I know we've only been going out for four months, but we've both decided – this is it. Right, Rose?'

'Yes. This is it.'

Mum tries to cut in before it gets serious.

'Now, Kevin, just a min –'

'No, Mum. We're going to get married. Before I go to Vietnam.'

'If we have your permission,' Rose adds.

'Go for it,' I tell them. 'Good one.'

'God,' Mum mutters, and she's not even praying.

Dad gives Rose a kiss on the cheek.

'You've got my permission, luv. Done! I've always liked you.' He looks at Mum, as if to say, 'Your turn now.'

Mum can't hide how she feels. Tears come and fall, though she tries to blink them away.

'Let me think, let me think. I wasn't expecting this. Maybe one day, but not tonight. I don't know what to say to you.'

'Would you like a cup of tea?' asks Dad. 'Might settle you down.'

Mum doesn't answer. Poor Dad. Sometimes he hasn't got a clue.

'All I want is for you to both be happy,' she says. 'But are you sure? It's such a huge commitment. You're so young – marriage is forever.'

Rose answers, quiet and simple: 'We love each other.'

Kevin nods. Rose frowns at him. She needs more than that.

It's a bit like watching how Mum and Dad work together.

'It's true,' he says, taking the hint, 'we do – we love each other.'

I think saying that out loud in front of us is pretty brave. But then he tops it. He kisses Rose square on the lips. No dainty aunty peck with Kevin. He goes in for the kill.

Mum looks away. Dad grins. I whistle high, then low.

I'm used to hearing Kevin's snores zigzag around our bedroom as soon as his head hits the pillow. This night there's only silence from his side of the room, though I know he's wide awake, same as me.

'How come you're not asleep?' I say.

'Because you're talkin' too much.'

'I've hardly said anything yet.'

'You will.'

'. . . That was good about you and Rose.'

'Thanks.'

'Hey, Kevin, you know about girls, right?'

He snorts.

'Well, you know more than I do.'

'Everyone knows more than you do, Neil. Even Dad.'

'Can I ask you somethin'?'

'If you have to.'

'There's this girl. She's older than me.'

'What is she – eighty – ninety?'

'Don't be stupid. She's five or six years older – I'm not sure exactly.'

'So? Dad's seven years older than Mum.'

'Is he? The dirty bugger. I didn't know that.'

'So she's not too old. Glad I could help. 'Night, Neil.'

'Hang on. I haven't finished.'

'Aw, stuff it . . . all right, I'm listenin'.'

'Well, she's a nurse and she's really pretty and smart. Sometimes I think she likes me, but then I'm not sure. She's out of my league, I know that, but I can't get her off my mind. What would you do?'

'Are you really my brother? Get real! You go for it, of course. Ask her out somewhere. What's the worst that can happen?'

'She could say she doesn't want to see me again.'

'Big deal. I'll tell you what – me weddin' – see if she wants to go.'

'No. I couldn't do that. I don't know her well enough.'

'Nee-il! All girls love weddin's. Deadset. It's like blokes and boobs. They can't help it. She'll go. Ask her tomorrow.'

'When's it on?'

'I don't know yet. Rose hasn't told me. Just tell her it's on *soon*.'

'Let me think about it.'

'What's to think about?'

'My future.'

'You won't have a future if I have to go over there and sort yer out. Come on! I'm goin' to Vietnam to get shot at. All you have to do is talk to a girl.'

'I'd trade with you if I could.'

'That's it! I've had it with you, Neil. I'm goin' to sleep. Don't say another word. And never ask me for advice again. You're hopeless!'

I say it so softly it's almost not there, but I say it. 'All right. I'll ask her.'

41

It's easy to find an excuse to go and see her. Sylvie tried to save my life at the dam – that deserves a thank-you present.

I go into a shop and check out my options. There's a droopy bunch of flowers for four dollars. But then I'd have to carry them all the way to her flat. Carrying flowers in public doesn't appeal to me. Another possibility is a box of el cheapo chocolates. Hmm . . .

Here's a box of chocolates for trying to save my life.

No. It doesn't seem like a fair trade.

There is one last possibility . . .

I buy her a card. It has two cute bear cubs on the front – real ones, not cartoons – and absolutely no mushy writing.

The last time I had a try at this I couldn't get any further than *Dear Sylvie*, but I know her better now so it shouldn't be too difficult.

Here I go again:

Dear Sylvie
Thanks for saving my life – it wasn't worth saving
before I met you.
Neil
X

As soon as I've written it I start swearing at myself. She's never going to see that card. I go out of my way to get one without mushy writing and then I turn into King Mush himself. Idiot!

I buy the same card again. This time I play it safe.

Dear Sylvie
I'm sure I thanked you for saving me at the dam,
but I wanted to thank you again.
Neil.
PS I hope you like bears.

That's perfect. No mush. And not an X in sight.

I listen outside her flat. I've already decided that if there's a bloke inside with her this time, then I'm knocking at the wrong door – I'll go and I won't come back. But all I hear is a vacuum cleaner grinding away at full blast. It takes a few loud knocks before the cleaner is switched off and Sylvie opens the door.

'Oh. Hello, Neil.'

It hardly looks like her. Her face is almost plain. The rims of her eyes are red and wet.

Ignoring all that, I hand her the card.

'I wanted to buy you a proper present,' I say, 'but I didn't have enough money to get you something decent, so I bought you a card. It's pretty ordinary – I just wanted you to know I was grateful for what you did at the dam.'

'Please come in. I'm a bit of a fright at the moment – no make-up. I worked night shift and I haven't been up very long.'

'Maybe I should go and let you get some sleep.'

'Don't you dare go. I'll make you a cup of tea – I want one myself. Do you drink tea?'

'Yep.' I walk inside. 'At our house we have it coming out of the taps – just about anyway.'

She opens the card and smiles at the bears. That's hopeful. Then she reads the message and smiles again.

'That's sweet of you, Neil. And it's not an ordinary card. It's lovely . . .'

I listen for any warning signs in her voice as we talk. Is she irritated, annoyed, fed up with me? No. Unless she's hiding it really well.

It's now or never.

'Sylvie, my brother Kevin is getting married.'

'That's exciting. Great.'

'I don't know when it is yet, but it's soon – he's been called up for the war.'

'Right. And he wants to get married before he goes?'

'That's the plan.'

'Well, I think that's a good idea. Congratulate him for me.'

'I will. Um, he said I could bring someone to the wedding, so' – this is absolute torture – 'I was wondering if you'd like to go with me.'

'You're inviting me? Well . . . That's a surprise.'

Now I hear the warning signs. I've probably embarrassed her. Got to get out of this – for her sake as well as mine.

'Yeah, on second thoughts, it's probably not a very good idea. I didn't think it through properly – you're working long hours and you're busy and you won't know anyone there – I'm only going 'cause I have to. It was a spur of the moment thing to ask you, so . . . maybe we should just forget about it – I'll save you some cake.'

'Don't you want to hear my answer?'

'Not really . . . It depends on what you're going to say. I don't want you to feel like you have to be nice to me.'

'I always have a good time at weddings, Neil. I'm glad that you asked me. I'd be honoured to go with you.'

'Really? You sure? Because you don't have to – you're not going to hurt my feelings or anything.'

'I'm sure.'

I know when she bites her bottom lip that she's going to cry. We both pretend it's not happening.

'I'll put the kettle on. Do you take milk?'

'Yes, thanks. You want any help?'

'No. I'm good.'

She's at the cupboards with her back to me, wiping her eyes with a hanky, trying not to let me see what is so obvious.

'You okay, Sylvie?'

Still with her back to me, she shakes her head.

I always thought I'd be clueless in any kind of situation with a girl. But instinct kicks in and I walk over and put my arm around her shoulder. It's something I couldn't do at the movies but now it feels completely natural.

'What's wrong?'

She faces me, tears welling in her eyes.

'It's Dad. He went for tests last week – he's had a sore throat for a long time now – Mum rang a little while ago with the results. I've just told Ray. He's taking it hard . . .'

That's as far as she can go.

I don't even feel scared as I hug her.

'Nothing's going to happen for a while. It might take a year. The doctors say there's no point in operating on him. It's gone too far.'

Her chin rests on my shoulder. I feel her tears on my neck.

'When you work in a hospital, Neil, you see so many people who have to go through this – being told what will happen.'

I do listen and I care, but I've never been so close to a girl before.

'You always think you're immune to it – that somehow it can't get to you, and even if it does, you'll handle it – but then it hits your own family, and you're a heaving mess, just like everybody else.'

I take the big risk and touch her face. I can't compare it to anything. Nothing else is so warm and smooth. I'm like an alien who's never made human contact before. And I can't get enough.

'Neil.'

My hand glides in a circle around her cheek.

'What are you doing?'

'Nothing.'

Now my fingers slowly flit across her mouth. She arches her neck. I trace a line around her nose . . . touch her eyes.

She clasps my wrist firmly. 'We can't do this.'

Then she presses my hand against her face and holds it there. It feels like there's a fight going on inside her.

She says, 'No' and so I keep still. I wait.

Closing her eyes, she guides my hand.

Then I start shaking.

We lie there tangled up in our own thoughts. After being almost one person, now we're nearly strangers again. I don't know what she's thinking, but for me it's about capturing every detail: the date and the hour; the Beatles singing 'Yesterday', with the radio turned down to almost nothing; my fumbles and embarrassments – I must have set some kind of record – and her every word, every look, every shudder . . . every bit of hope she gave me.

All these years I've had the Brothers telling me about miracles, but they never mentioned this one. I feel sorry for them.

'It's okay, Neil. It's okay. Don't worry. It's only me.'

She whispered that, looking up at me and trusting. There was nothing but kindness in her eyes, and even now, she's still holding my hand.

42

Sylvie sits up and gives me a kiss on the forehead. 'You have to go. I'm sorry.' She hops out of bed, clutching a sheet around her. 'I have a lot of things to do, and you should be getting home.'

I don't understand what's going on. Everything's changed, so fast. It shouldn't end like this – should it?

'I'll have a quick shower and then if you want I can drive you home.'

I have to know what she's thinking.

'Did I do something wrong, Sylvie?'

She comes back and sits on the edge of the bed.

'No. Don't be silly. I'm not trying to get rid of you. I really do have a lot to do. Mum and Dad are expecting me but before that I have to go and see Ray. He's still cut off from Dad and that's really going to hurt him now.'

'Ray'll be all right. He's tougher than you think.'

'Yeah? I wish I could be so sure. He tries to hide it, but I know he's still churned up about being expelled from school ... do you think he might do something to that Principal he fought with? He told me once that he would. The second he saw that I was concerned he wouldn't talk about it anymore.'

That hits me hard. It's bad enough screwing up Zom's life, but now Sylvie's been dragged into this thing too.

'No, he wouldn't do anything,' I lie. 'Don't worry, Sylvie. I'll go and sort him out – make sure he's okay.'

She leans over and kisses me gently on the lips.

'Thanks, Neil.'

The shower beats down as I get dressed; a commercial blares on the radio. It's hard to believe my world has shifted so much, on such an ordinary day.

When Sylvie steps out of the bathroom I tell her I'll pass up the ride home.

'It's not far to walk,' I say. 'Anyway, I've got some thinking to do. It's been a big day.'

'Okay then. Well, I'll ring you, all right?'

'Yeah. That'd be great.'

I get one last hug, and then I'm at the door, grinning like a dork who just found the golden needle in a haystack.

'Hey . . .'

'Yep?'

'. . . You were great, Neil.'

It's the sort of lie nice people *have* to say.

But I could love someone for a lie like that.

43

Friday nights usually zoom. This one staggers along on crutches.

I watch TV with Mum and Dad. There are about ten machine-gun killings during *The Untouchables* and Dad sleeps through the lot. I worry about him sometimes. Hanging up in his wardrobe there's a suit he's picked out to wear at his own funeral. Looking at him now, it's like he's practising for the grave. I think that's what I've been doing too. Until today.

Mum's knitting needles click away feverishly. She makes shawls and blankets for poor people. If all her work was put together there'd be a blanket big enough to fit over the Great Wall of China.

All my Friday nights have been like this, wrapped up safe and warm in the family cocoon. It's never bothered me before but tonight I'm restless. I wander around the house, lie on my bed, thinking. Be good if Troy was here. I wonder if I'd tell him? Probably not. I'd just smile a lot and he'd guess . . . I jump up after a few minutes and go outside to play with Dusty. I don't know what I want – maybe just to be some place where I can yell at the top of my voice, a riotous, untamed noise to tell the world that I don't feel like a schoolboy anymore. I know I've got a way to go before I can say I'm a man, but at least now I reckon I'm officially alive.

Back inside, in front of the TV again, Mum looks up from her knitting.

'Is everything all right, Neil?'

'Yep. Couldn't be better.'

I sit there and do my best to act normal, but it's a tough trick when your heart's just been shocked out of a lifetime sleep.

The only trophy I own is for soccer. I sat on the reserve bench for the whole season and my feet didn't touch the grass once. Probably because I left them alone, my team won the premiership and I got to collect my prized award.

I deserve another trophy for today's effort – Best and Fairest Virgin, that sounds about right . . . Most Desperate? Most Bloody Grateful? I don't know, but there should be some way of marking the day as special. I want a way to remember so in twenty years I can look back on today and say 'Something Happened Here.'

Maybe Kevin will celebrate with me. We can drink Dad's home brew and dance around the house naked. Or maybe he'll just talk to me . . .

He lobs home late after a night out with Rose, mumbles 'Goodnight,' but doesn't turn the light on, or bother about getting changed. Even his shoes stay on him as he flops face-down onto the bed like a worn-out sack of spuds.

'Kev.'

'I'm asleep.'

'Okay. Forget it.'

'All right – tell me quick.'

'Um . . . I don't know where to start.'

He sits up in the bed and flicks on the light.

'This better be good. I'm listenin'.'

No. I can't do it. We haven't had enough practice at being brothers. Maybe when we're old blokes it will be easier to talk and be close.

'It doesn't matter,' I tell him. 'Wasn't important.'

'Bloody hell!'

He snaps the light off and lies back down.

'I know somethin's up with ya, Neil. Tell me.'

In the darkness I sort out my words – groping, stumbling words – what I really need is Sylvie to put her arms around me and then I wouldn't have to say anything. Now everything is just a logjam; thoughts, feelings, words, a logjam stuck deep in my heart. Only one thing is clear. Dad says you can't live on dreams. Wrong. Tonight I can.

'I'm asleep,' I say.

44

Sylvie rings me in the morning. From the first words she says, I know something's wrong.

'I took Ray to visit Dad last night. I thought now that he's sick it would be different. But Dad got upset and started yelling. Then he couldn't stop coughing. Mum was crying. It was horrible, and Ray was in the middle of it all. He just took off, Neil – wouldn't let me take him home. He failed his driver's licence too, so he's miserable about that. I'm so worried about him. I know he's working at the newspaper this morning. I have to drive to Newcastle for the baptism of a friend's baby so I won't be able to see him today. I was wondering if you –'

'Sure, Sylvie. I'm on my way right now.'

The *Leader* is closed on weekends but I notice a fan whirring inside. I knock on the glass door and soon Zom comes out to open up.

'Sylvie sent you here, didn't she?'

'She didn't *send* me. She just said you had a bad time last night with your dad – she's worried about you.'

He gestures for me to come in, and when I do he closes the door behind us.

'I know you're trying to help, Neil. I'm just a bit on edge today.'

'Not a problem. I'm sorry your dad is sick.'

Zom's never on edge, so I know something's up.

'Have you ever been in a newspaper office before?'

'No. First time.'

'I'll show you around. I need a minute to think about what to say to you.'

'Suits me.'

I follow as he walks through the building.

'This is where the journos work.'

I see three desks weighed down by massive type-writers. The wastebaskets are flowing over with crumpled-up paper.

Here the editor's office.

There are the sales reps.

'And this is the darkroom. Mind your head.'

A tablecloth would almost cover the room. Black and whites are pegged up to dry, same as clothes that have just been washed. One whole wall is covered with photos. Most were taken by the paper's main photographer. Zom points to his own efforts, the way some parents show off the pictures of their babies.

'You like this job, don't you, Zom?'

'Yes, I do. It's . . .' He pauses to straighten up a photo. 'It's like the first place I've really belonged.'

'Then why would you want to stuff things up when they're going so good? Wouldn't it just be easier to draw a line through Mick and forget him?'

He shrugs, the way I have so many thousand times. It drives my mum crazy and now I have some idea why.

In the staff room, he goes to a fridge, opens it and holds up a bottle.

'Lemonade?'

'For sure.'

I take a chair. He sits at a desk.

'Sorry you missed out on your licence,' I say.

'Doesn't matter.' Big sigh from him . . . 'Brother Michael – is that what you're here about?'

'You know it is. You're always going on about doing something to him and now you've got Sylvie believing you really mean it.'

'I shouldn't have said anything to her. I only said it once.'

'You shouldn't tell anyone, Zom. It's a load of bull and you know it. Just get on with your life and forget about Mick. He's a mean bastard – so what? The world is full of them.'

'Neil. I'm telling you because you're my friend. And I need to talk to someone . . . Sylvie worrying about me isn't going to make any difference. Now I know exactly what I'm going to do. Brother Michael is not going to live longer than my father.'

'That's garbage. No one kills a Brother.'

'He disgraced me and my family. I lost my father's respect because of him. I was always going to do it. But after last night I want it more than ever.'

'Zom, mate –'

'It's tonight, Neil.'

45

I give him a lecture my mum would be proud of.

'You do this and it's going to wreck your life. You'll end up in jail, Zom – bring even more disgrace to your family. What's your dad going to think of you then?'

'No, no.' He purses his lips and briskly shakes his head. 'It won't be like that.'

'It will. Believe me, it will.'

'You want to hear it, Neil? What I'm going to do? Because all along you've known, you should know now. I trust you.'

'No, don't tell me. I don't want to be part of it – and you shouldn't trust me.'

He hops up from the desk and stands in front of me.

'Of course I trust you. You're the only one from school who cared anything about me when I was expelled. I'll never forget that.'

I sink into the chair. I feel like sinking into the floor. Zom deserves a real friend, not me.

'All right, tell me,' I say, 'and then I'll tell you why it won't work.'

'Okay.' He nods. 'Only you, Neil. I'm telling only you.'

He drops to the carpet, sitting cross-legged.

'It's a simple plan. There are two parts to it: first I steal a car, then I drive the car at Brother Michael. I hit him and I keep on going.'

He says it cold and clinical – detached, like it's not a flesh and blood person he's talking about.

'It isn't,' he says when I tell him that. 'It's Brother Michael.'

As he fills in the details I try to pull the plan to pieces but every thread is stitched up tight.

He knows how to break into a car – how to hotwire it.

'I've met some police since I've been on the paper. Been over at the station a few times to take their photos. I ask lots of questions. Sooner or later someone gives me the answers I want.'

He knows that every night just before 7 pm Mick goes for a walk on his own – always takes the same roads.

'In the street where I'm going to do it, there are

only factories. No one works there on the weekends.'

He'll be wearing gloves so there won't be any finger-prints. And he's already got the car picked out, and the place where he's going to ditch it.

'I'll be back in my flat in an hour,' Zom says, 'and when it's done, I won't miss any sleep.'

46

He's still the same Zom I know, except now he's talking like a killer and it doesn't bother him. I can only think of one way to change his mind. It's got to be the hardest thing I've ever done.

'Zom, it's me you should kill.'

He looks at me curiously. 'What do you mean?'

I decided a long time ago that if it ever came to this, Troy wouldn't be part of it.

'The wallet that Mick blamed you for stealing – I'm the one who took it.'

It's as if I've told him some weird joke that he's struggling to understand. He almost smiles.

'I never wanted you to get into any trouble. I was playing a trick on Paul Burke, that's all – nicked the wallet, meant to give it back – but before I could, Mick was belting into you. I should have said something straightaway. I was too scared. I was gutless, Zom.'

The silence coming off him fills up the whole room. It crushes me.

'Hit me. Do whatever you want. I mean it. I've got it coming. I told you not to trust me. Bloody hit me!'

'That's the only thing I'm sure of. I won't hit you, Neil.' He stands, his arms folded. 'I've only hit one person in my life – Brother Michael. You're not the same as him ... I knew someone had to have it done it, but I never once thought it was you.'

'You must hate me. You should. I screwed up your life.'

He ponders that, but not for long.

'No. I could never hate you.'

'Is that it? You're not going to do anything?'

'Because of this I've come to know you, Neil. It might have started off bad, but you've been looking out for me ever since. No matter what, I think of you as my friend.'

'Even after everything I've done to you?'

'You made a mistake. I understand how it happened. You didn't mean to hurt me. It's all right.'

'Zom, there's only one thing you should understand: I watched you going under and I didn't lift a finger to help. Don't kill Mick for something that I did. I'm responsible. I'm the one who should pay, and I will – any way you want.'

His hands are knitted together. They rest under his chin, his eyes lowered; always thinking, Zom.

'All right, Neil. You can repay your debt.'

'What do you want me to do?'

'There's one weakness in my plan. When I steal the car it will take me a few minutes to get it started. That's the only time I'm vulnerable. Stand at the back of the car. Whistle if someone comes. That's all you have to do. You've been with me all along, Neil, one way or another. Do this and then we're even.'

47

Any other time I'd have laughed if someone said that to me, but Zom is too serious to laugh at. He waits for an answer and I know it needs to be a good one. It can't just be a flat 'no'. I have to offer him something.

'I've got a better idea, Zom. Will you listen to it?'

'All right then.'

'I'll go to Mick today – now – and I'll confess everything. I stole the wallet. I'll tell him straight. You had nothing to do with it.'

'He'll strap you.'

'Too bad. It's what I should have got from the start. But I'll clear your name, Zom. I'll tell him your dad's sick and I'll get him to phone him. I can make everything all right again. I know I can.'

He nods, mulling it over like he always does. I haven't got time for that. If I don't go to see Mick right now, I never will.

'Do we have a deal, Zom? If I can fix this you'll give up the idea of killing Mick – once and for all. What do you say?'

'Yes. Okay.' He offers his hand for me to shake. I give him mine. 'If this works I'll forget Brother Michael once and for all.' The handshake is over but he still clenches my hand. 'But if it doesn't work, Neil, you help me to steal the car, just like I said. That's the only deal I'll agree to. What do *you* say?'

48

I catch the bus up the hill, as if it's just another school day, dreading every second. I want to get off and run and hide but I'll be doing that all my life unless I make a stand now. I think of how Mick slammed into Zom that day when he thought he'd stolen the wallet. Now it's my turn. I have to keep telling myself, over and over like a prayer, that no matter what Mick does to me, this is the right thing to do.

It's the first time I've ever gone to the Brothers' house. Just knocking on the door feels like a sin. Clementian answers. I hardly recognise him without the black habit. He's wearing shorts and a white T-shirt. He looks ordinary.

'What are you doing here, Bridges?'

'I came to see Brother Michael, if I could, Bra. If it's all right.'

He looks annoyed. That's not unusual.

'Wait here.'

I'm standing on the verandah. My lips are dry and so is my tongue – but I'm sweating.

Clementian lumbers back out.

'Brother will see you in his office.'

I follow him inside, down a long dark hallway. Brother Geoffrey watches car racing on TV. Johnno's in the kitchen. He looks up at me and smiles – he'll never know how important that smile is. Sometimes all you need is one smile.

'Here he is, Brother Michael.'

'Come.'

Clementian waves me inside and shuts the door behind him as he leaves. Mick is writing something in a notebook. Even today he's wearing his habit. He doesn't look up.

The room is crammed with heavy books tightly squeezed together. Everywhere there are photos related to school: sporting teams, captains and prefects, decades-old classes where the faces have almost disappeared.

'Are you going to speak or not?' Mick lifts his head at last. 'I am very busy here. Why have you come to see me on a Saturday morning?'

'Sorry to bother you, Brother Michael. I wouldn't have come if it wasn't important. There's something I have to tell you.'

He puts his pen down, and waits.

'It's about that time with Ray Zeeba – when he was expelled. There was a wallet that went missing.'

'It was stolen if my memory serves me correctly – by Mr Zeeba.'

'That's the thing, Brother, it wasn't him . . . I stole the wallet.'

'You?'

'Yes. I only meant it as a joke – I wasn't going to keep it. Then when Ray got into trouble I was too scared to admit what I'd done.'

'You stole the wallet?'

'That's right.'

'And why are you coming forward at this late stage?'

'Ray's father is sick. I think he might be dying.'

'I'm sorry to hear that. But what has it got to do with this wallet business? Try to make yourself clear, will you?'

'His father kicked him out of the house, Brother – because he hit you. And now his father's sick and he's still not talking to Ray. They might not see each other again.'

'That is a family matter. It has nothing to do with me.'

'I thought if I owned up to what I'd done, you could ring Ray's father and tell him it was all right now – tell him that Ray was innocent the whole time.'

'Well, well. I see. It's very good of you to work all this out for me, Bridges. Isn't it?'

I don't know what the right answer is so I look at the floor.

He stands up and reaches into his pocket. The long, deep pocket where he keeps the strap.

'Perhaps I should simply ask you what I should do in future. Consult Mr Bridges before I make decisions? Do you think?'

'I don't know, Brother.'

I see the strap now. He places it on the desk beside him.

'The sin of omission is every bit as bad as a lie. You know that much, don't you?'

'Yes, Brother.'

He stands in front of me, his hands behind his back, his chest out. He knows how to make himself bigger when he wants to make you feel smaller.

'As well as that you have been cowardly. Is that a fair statement?'

'It's fair.'

'Finally, you are a thief. Say it.'

'I'm a thief, Brother.'

'Aren't you lucky that God loves sinners . . . hmm?'

'Um . . . Yes, Brother.'

'And even luckier that I'm in a good mood. On your knees.'

I hesitate.

'Well? I don't mean tomorrow! Get on your knees!'

As I kneel he creaks down beside me, the rosary beads spilling over the tops of his hands.

'Come on, Bridges. Help me pray for your soul – Our Father who art in Heaven,' he glares at me until I chant it with him, 'hallowed be Thy name. Thy kingdom come. Thy will be done, on Earth as it is in Heaven . . .'

When he gets to 'Amen' he stands and brushes the dirt from his habit, then eases himself down again at his desk.

'Move along, lad. You're not going to park yourself there all day.'

I jump up quickly.

'Now this is what we'll do. For the next week you'll pick up papers for a half an hour twice a day, at lunchtime and after school. And you can consider yourself a very fortunate young fellow.'

'Yes, Brother.'

'Off you go then. And don't let me see you back here.'

I stay.

'Brother?'

'I said you can go. Something wrong with your ears? Run along.'

'Yes, Brother . . . but . . .'

'What do you want, Bridges?'

'Will you ring up Ray's father? If he hears it from you he'll change his mind. He'll let Ray come home. I've got the number right here.'

I offer him the piece of paper but he doesn't look at it.

'My boy, now you are trying my patience. What happens with Mr Zeeba and his father is none of my concern. Or yours. That matter is closed. Clean the wax out of your ears. It is closed! Now go home, Bridges – and don't waste my time again.'

49

On the bus back into town I think about miracles. Mick will strap you any time for looking at him the wrong way or just because he feels like it, but today he lets me go. He must be going soft in his old age, or maybe he just likes to keep his victims guessing. Whatever the reason, it's got to be damn close to a miracle. I don't like the chances of getting two of them in one day. I made a deal with Zom and I can't take it back. I have to be his lookout when he steals the car. But one thing about the church, it teaches you not to give up . . .

Please help me find a way out of this, God. Give me one more miracle.

I don't even have to tap on the door. Zom is standing right there waiting for me.

'Did you see him, Neil?'

'Yeah, I did.'

He studies my face for only a moment and knows what happened.

'He's not going to ring my father, is he?'

'No. I'm sorry. I tried hard.'

'I didn't think he would. Thanks for giving it a shot.'

'Look, Zom, what about if I go and see your dad? I'll tell him what I did – I'll tell anyone you want.'

'My father might have listened to a school principal, but what you or I say doesn't mean anything to him. Anyway, it doesn't matter. After tonight no one will be hurt by Brother Michael, ever again.'

'Please don't do it.'

'Are you with me, Neil?'

'You can't kill someone, Zom. No matter what he did to you.'

'Forget me. What about all the ones that come after me? I've thought about this so much. He made me hate. Do I let him do that again? When you see something that's evil, do you turn your back?'

'I don't know – but you haven't got the right to decide. It's murder – the worst sin of all.'

'That's true. But tonight I'm going to stop believing in sin. Until it's over, all I believe in is justice. Are you with me?'

'God, Zom.'

'You shook my hand.'

'This is wrong.'

'Neil?'

If I go with him at least there's a chance I can stop him – and with or without me, he's determined to go ahead with it.

'Yes,' I answer. 'I'm with you.'

50

'We should stay together all day,' Zom says. 'I don't want to be looking for you at the last minute.'

I tell him I'll have to ring home and let Mum know everything's okay – otherwise she'll worry.

'Good idea. Say you don't know what you're doing yet, but you're with a friend from school.'

'Okay.'

'And then we'll go to a movie. *Bonnie and Clyde* is on at the Vista.'

'I don't get you, Zom. You're talking about killing someone tonight and you want to go to a movie today. It doesn't make sense.'

'We need to fill in time, Neil. And there's another reason. When you get home your mother is going to want to know what you've been doing all day. Am I right?'

'Probably.'

'You had lunch, you talked, you walked – and you went to a movie. All true. Make the call.'

I do it, just like Zom wants.

'Take care,' Mum says. 'Don't be home late.'

As I'm about to hang up I tell her I love her. I mumble it low so she can hardly hear me, but whether she hears or not, I need to say it.

Zom buys me lunch at the shopping centre cafeteria. Afterwards he leaves me alone while he goes to the toilet. I'm on the top floor, leaning against a rail with about a hundred-foot drop in front of me. The hardest part would be climbing up on the rail and letting myself go. Closing my eyes, I see myself falling. It would be almost like I was flying. That would be the last thing I'd know – I'd be flying. That's one way out of this. I'm too chicken to do it, of course, but I reckon just thinking about it is a kind of death.

'Neil. It's time to go.'

'This here's Bonnie Parker. I'm Clyde Barrow. We rob banks.'

I love everything about this movie, except the ending. I hate it when you get to like someone and they're killed in the last scene. All the rest of the movie you can laugh at but it's too real and sad at the end when Bonnie and Clyde are shot about a million times in slow motion. Maybe I'll see it again when all this stuff with Mick is over and I don't have to worry about anyone dying in real life.

After the movie Zom takes me to his flat so he can pick up the tools he needs to steal the car. I don't try to change his mind because I know he won't listen anymore. He's doing it. No matter what.

'There it is.'

We look down from a railway bridge at a black Ford sedan.

'The man who owns it manages the bowling alley across the road,' Zom tells me. 'I used to be in a team that played there every week.'

'Why that car?'

'I've done my research: it's an easy one to steal, automatic, no alarm, no steering lock.'

'You've got it all worked out.'

'And I've been around the manager enough to know what he's like. He puts his wife down in front of other people, treats his staff badly – he deserves to lose something. Any other questions?'

'No. Yes. One thing. It's only five o'clock now. You said Mick goes walking at seven. Can't we wait a while longer? Can't we just talk some more?'

'I got here early so you could be home well before it happened – then you can't be implicated.'

'But what will you do for two hours?'

'I'll sit and think about Brother Michael and what he did. I need to do that, one last time.'

'Okay.'

'Then we go.'

He races ahead of me down the steps. My legs turn to jelly. He wheels around and urges me on.

'I don't think I can go through with this, Zom.'

'You can.'

He keeps going. I feel like I've got to follow him.

'Stand here.' He positions me near the car boot. 'If anyone comes, you whistle once and then you get out of here.' He grabs my shoulders and squeezes down on them. 'Two minutes and I'm done. Two minutes and you walk away. Are you up for this, Neil?'

Troy comes into my mind. I see him dead on the road. I think about all the times he was strapped.

Two minutes and you walk away . . .

'Yeah, I am. Just do it.'

Zom prises open a window. He's inside the car and working under the steering wheel, near the ignition lock. I'm not supposed to look suspicious – have to be casual. How do you do that when your heart is almost out of your chest and bouncing down the street?

I stare at my watch. Thirty seconds. A minute.

Hurry up.

Two minutes-thirty now.

'What are you doing?'

No answer.

Across the road a car door slams. A police car. Two cops get out.

I can't make myself whistle.

'Zom. Zom.'

They haven't seen us yet but they're heading this way.

'Zom!'

He starts up the Ford and calmly backs it out. Stopping beside me, he winds down the driver's window.

'I see them, Neil. Go home.'

'No, wait –'

'There isn't time.'

The Ford slips past me out onto the road. Zom hunches over the wheel, so grimly determined, and drives off.

There isn't going to be another miracle today.

51

Our house smells like Saturday: Mum is cooking dinner, Kevin's footy socks are on the floor stinking up our bedroom.

Mum looks pointedly at her watch, but skips the speech.

'Did you have a nice time with your friend?'

'It was okay.'

'That's good . . . what did you do all day?'

'Just hung around – talked, had lunch, saw this movie – *Bonnie and Clyde* – it was about these two bank robbers . . .'

Zom got it so right. It's good to be able to answer honestly, and after I finish telling Mum about the movie, there are no more questions.

I set the table for three – Kevin is at Rose's place tonight – then it's my turn to say grace. The words are automatic, like the ten times tables.

Ten ones are ten . . .

Bless us, oh Lord, and these your gifts, which we are about to receive from your bounty. Through Christ our Lord –

I hold back the last word for a second so Mum and Dad can chime in –

Amen.

. . . Ten tens are a hundred.

Soon we've eaten and washed up, the plates are stacked away.

Mum sits at the kitchen table to write down her life in the journal.

Dad goes out to the shed to be Van Gogh.

For a little while I throw the ball for Dusty – because she loves it so much – and then I hide out in my room and wait for Zom's phone call.

I hear the underneath things: clocks ticking, a bird skittering across the tin roof, the fridge doing its endless death rattle, the wind whirring in the distance. Clearest of all, I hear my conscience.

There's still time to ring the police or the Brothers – warn them.

If I let this happen, I'm a murderer too.

I don't move off the bed.

* * *

It's seven o'clock.

Zom will probably be parked down a side street with the engine ticking away, just waiting for Mick to wander into the trap.

It might be happening right now.

Every minute I spend thinking about it is a little piece of agony.

'I'll get that.'

It's 8 pm and the phone is ringing.

'No, Mum. I've got it.'

I run like mad to get there before her.

'Yes?'

'Neil.'

It's only Kevin.

'Yeah.'

'Turn on the TV. Channel 7. There's gunna be somethin' on about Brother Mick from the school.'

'What happened to him?'

'No idea – I just came into the room in time to hear his name. They said the full story's comin' up in the news after the ad break . . .'

I drop the phone.

52

In breaking news, a school principal is being hailed as a hero tonight after rescuing a teenage boy from a wrecked car, shortly before it burst into flames.

A word spews out of my mouth that this house has never heard. It brings Mum running into the room.

'Neil! What is the –'

She stops when she sees me staring at the screen as someone is being loaded into an ambulance.

'What's wrong, Neil?'

'It's Ray.'

'The boy you were with today?'

'Yes – yes.'

I'm only dimly aware of Mum taking my hand but the newsreader's every word drills through me sharp and clear.

Witnesses say Brother Michael Evans showed no concern for his own safety as . . .

Police allege . . .

A sixteen-year-old boy . . .

Driving too fast . . .

Lost control on a corner . . .

Serious condition at Grogan Hospital.

Mum switches off the TV.

'We'll leave now,' she says.

We follow the signs, take the lift to the second floor, and soon we're at the information desk of the hospital. Mum and Dad and me.

I ask about Zom but I call him Ray. 'How is he? Can I see him?'

The woman at the desk searches for his file, and finds it.

'Are you related to the patient?'

'I'm his friend – he'd want to see me.'

She glances at Mum and Dad, eyebrows slightly raised.

'We're all family friends,' Dad lies. 'Very close.'

Mum stabs him with a disapproving glare but he ignores it.

The woman leans forward and points towards the back wall.

'You go straight through those blue doors.'

53

Inside the waiting room there are eight or nine members of Zom's family. I only know it's them because I see his mother. His father's not there – and I don't see Sylvie. She's on her way, someone says. I remember what she told me this morning – *driving to Newcastle...*

Mum introduces herself to everyone, moving from one handshake to the next until she gets to Zom's mother. She crouches beside her, clasps her hand when she gets teary, pats her back, talks softly, listens to every word.

The two of us are so different. Mum can hug and cry easily with people who are strangers. Not me. I feel a lot of things about Zom tonight but I don't let any of them out.

Two cops arrive. They hang around in corners like unwanted pot plants, keeping their distance from Zom's family. One catches a nurse's attention as she goes by. They exchange whispers before he shows her the name written in his notebook. She nods and I hear the word 'critical'. They leave without speaking to anyone else. I'm sure they'll come back but I'm not worried about Zom getting into trouble over the stolen car. He's got bigger problems than that.

Shortly after they leave a doctor walks in to see us.

'Zeeba?' she asks. 'The Zeeba family?'

'Yes.'

I hold my breath. I think we all do.

She goes into a huddle with Zom's mum at first, but realising her English is a problem she says it out loud, to all of us.

'Raymond was falling in and out of consciousness at the accident scene but he's stabilised now and his vital signs are positive.'

Some cry and others smile. Mum closes her eyes and mutters something under her breath – I know she's thanking God.

Before anyone can get too excited, the doctor continues. I hone in on the key words – *concussion, internal bleeding, not out of danger yet.*

She gives a tight-lipped smile that seems to say, *Don't get your hopes up.* 'I'll let you know as soon as I can about any changes to his condition.' Then there's a slight bob of her head, and she strides away.

54

It's a steaming night. We're all wiping away sweat. Zom's mum fans her face with a magazine. Used paper water cups pile up in the bin. Every time the door of the operating room opens we peer in trying to see Zom. Beyond the doctors and nurses, all I glimpse are machines and tubes. Patients and beds are a blur of white. The door closes too quickly.

It's close to ten when Sylvie arrives.

'Sylvana!'

Her mother rushes to her with arms wide. Relatives flock around to bring her up to date with news about Zom. She has a hug for every one of them. I stay well back with Mum and Dad.

Seeing her there has me spinning. I've got this great jumble of thoughts and feelings. We made love. I want to hold her. But how does she feel about me? I can't let my parents know about her. She mightn't want *anyone* to know about me. And what about Zom? How can I think about me when he's –

'Neil.'

Sylvie sees me and as soon as she can, she breaks away from the pack, comes over and kisses me on the cheek. It's just an ordinary kiss hello.

'Your brother's in our prayers,' Mum says.

'We're very sorry,' mutters Dad.

Sylvie whispers to me, 'Let's go outside, where it's quiet.'

We walk out to the machine in the foyer. I buy her a coffee and we sit on green plastic chairs. The room is empty apart from us.

She gets straight down to it.

'Do you know how this happened, Neil?'

I pause too long. I'm not such a good liar that I can do it instantly. She notices and goes after me.

'When I rang you this morning I told you I was worried about Ray, didn't I?'

'That's right – and I went to see him as soon as I hung up the phone.'

'Then what happened?'

I tell her the bits and pieces that I think are safe, but I hate it because every question chases me further down a dead end. I can only stall and dodge so long. Eventually I'll get to the part where I have to admit that I helped her brother steal the car that he crashed.

And then it's over for me and Sylvie. If I tell the truth, it's over.

'I don't understand, Neil. You say you were with Ray from early in the morning.'

'From after you rang, yeah. We saw a movie.'

'I don't care about the movie. If you were with him all day you must have some idea what he was doing in a stolen car just after he left you. You *must*.'

'Sylvie, I wasn't there when it crashed. I didn't know anything about that until I saw it on the TV news.'

'All right! You weren't there – but *before* that, when you *were* there – did he talk about it? Did he say anything at all that made you suspect he might steal a car?'

'Um – I don't think so.'

'You don't think so? . . . Christ!'

She gets set to backhand the cup of hot coffee – doesn't do it – does it. The cup flies across the room and coffee sprays in all directions.

'This isn't a little boy's game, Neil! My brother is lying on an operating table in there. He might not survive. Tell me what you know and don't stuff me around!'

'I tried all day to talk him out of it – he wouldn't listen to me.'

'Talk him out of what? Stealing the car?'

I've reached that dead end now. There's nowhere else to run.

'There's more to it than that, Sylvie.'

'Then tell me. I want to know everything there is to know.'

Not many people get the truth out of me these days – I think I've almost forgotten how to tell it – but Sylvie deserves at least that much from me. One piece on its own doesn't add up so I give her the bright shining *truth*, right back to where it all began, with the wallet – when I stole it, alone.

She listens, shaking her head, eyes closed. When it's finally done she stands and walks back towards the waiting room without a word to me.

'Sylvie, I'm sorry.' I don't try to stop her because I know she doesn't want me near her. 'I didn't mean any of this. Ray really is my friend.'

'No, you're not his friend.' She doesn't stop walking. 'It's because of you that he's here. Just go.'

Sylvie opens the door, steps in, and slams it behind her.

55

I'm sitting in the gutter when Mum and Dad come out.

'What did you say to that poor girl?' demands Mum. 'She's very upset in there.'

I'm not going to explain another thing for as long as I live.

'It's personal.' That's all I say.

Mum splutters and squawks but Dad takes my side.

'Ease up, Margaret,' he says, 'the lad's upset, too. We'll work it out when we get home. He's a good kid, you know that. Anyway, this isn't the time to argue. Let's just be glad we've got our boy in one piece. Not everyone can say that tonight.'

'Yes.' She kisses Dad on the forehead. 'You're quite right.' She turns to me, back to being my kind mum. 'Sylvie said she doesn't want you inside – for whatever reason. I'll give you the keys and you can wait for us in the car.'

'I'll be out here too,' Dad says.

'Thanks,' I tell him, 'but I don't need you to babysit me.'

'Who said I was doing it for you? I'm just glad to get out of that joint.' He takes the keys from Mum. 'Hospitals give me the heebie-jeebies.'

Dad tries to get me talking.

'I think your mate will be all right. They can work wonders, those doctors.'

The words tumble down a deep hole and there's no echo.

He waits a while and then he has another crack at it.

'That Sylvie seems a good style of a lass – I didn't even know you and her were friends.'

I don't answer that one either but it doesn't put him off.

'Now I don't know what the story is between you two – you'll tell me when you're ready – but it takes me back to me young days, this kind of situation. I've had many a night like this with your mother. Before we got married. Yeah. I know what it feels like. We'd have a blue over somethin' – nearly always my fault – and she'd get on her high horse, call me for everything and then she'd storm off. There were times there when I thought I'd never live through it . . . but you do, matey, you do.'

'Dad, I don't want to talk about Sylvie. Okay? I don't want to talk about anything.'

'Fair enough.'

I don't think he has any idea how I feel. Even I don't know. I suppose I'll start feeling it more tomorrow, but tonight I'm just a block of wood with tears.

We sit in the darkness, me and my dad, the windows open in the hope of trapping any breeze that floats by. None does. And then a taxi pulls up behind us. An old bloke bustles out – he's short and strong – and I know him from somewhere. He sees me and comes over, leans into the window.

'I look for Emergency. You know where I find?'

'Sure.' I get out of the car. Telling him directions isn't going to work. Too complicated. 'I'll show you,' I say. 'This way.'

I take him up in the lift and through to the blue doors. 'It's in there.'

'Thank you, my friend.' He gives me a tired smile. 'I go see my son. He very sick boy. My Raymond.'

56

'I always knew you'd make it, Zom. You can't kill a zombie – right?'

'Looks that way, Neil.' His face is still bandaged but I can see the smile in his eyes.

It's a week since the crash. First time I've been allowed in to see him. There's so much to say ...

'I had to tell Sylvie what happened. I couldn't lie anymore. She knows everything, Zom.'

'It's all right. We've talked about it. I think she understands what I did.'

'What about what I did? Does she understand that?'

'Can't say, Neil. She didn't want to talk about you.'

I shrug as if it doesn't mean a thing. It does.

'Cheer up,' Zom says. 'Everything is good now.'

'You think so? What about the police and the stolen car?'

'I'll worry about that later. Whatever the price, I'll pay it. The main thing is that getting smashed up brought me and my father together again. He came to the hospital. He said I can come home, Neil . . . I didn't think that was possible.'

I know that in his own quiet way Zom's jumping up and down. It's all on the inside, but it's just as real.

'That's great. It really is. I know how much it means to you.'

'Thanks, Neil.'

'Zom, there's one thing I'm desperate to find out – you know what it is.'

A nurse puts her head around the door.

'I'll have to ask you to leave in five minutes. Doctor needs to do some more tests.'

'Not a problem,' I tell her. 'This bloke's boring me anyway.'

He waits for her to walk away . . .

'You want to know what happened that night?'

'Of course I do. I'm dying to know. Did you just go too fast and lose it before you could get him? Or did you change your mind at the last second and swerve away?'

'I've thought about it a lot, Neil. I remember being in the car and seeing Brother Michael walk onto the road – but then there's nothing.'

'What do you mean, *nothing*?'

'It's gone. I've forgotten it all. I saw Brother Michael in front of me, and my next memory is waking up in the hospital.'

'Jeez . . . and now Mick's a hero for saving you.'

'It looks that way.'

'Do you still want to run him down?'

'Part of me does. Like I said to you before, I think he's evil. But he saved my life – that changes things. And I've got my father back . . . that's all I ever wanted.'

The nurse appears at the doorway. She gives me a look that says 'Time's up'.

'Gotta go, Zom. I'll come back to see you again.'

He doesn't answer because he's staring out the window at a car that's just driven into the parking lot below.

Sylvie's here.

57

She's coming up the steps, I'm going down . . .

I thought about hiding in the toilets until she'd gone past, but I have to see her – even if turns out to be the last time.

We stop as we draw level.

'How are you, Neil?'

'Good. I'm good. Just saw Ray. Looks like he's doing okay now. It took a while.'

'I'm glad I ran into you. Talk with me a minute?'

'Okay.'

I sit next to her in the middle of the stairway.

Most people I know are slow starters when the hard stuff has to be said. Sylvie's like that now. When she sighs I want to put my arm around her. I think maybe she wants that, too. We could do this without any words. One look from her and I'd know everything was going to be all right. Instead I get a smile – not the toothpaste-ad kind – this is the one smile I don't want. I know it means *goodbye*.

'Give me your hand,' she says. 'I'll tell your future.'

'I don't want to know it.'

She takes my hand anyway.

The Brothers tell us that the big *M* everyone has on their palm is supposed to stand for Mary, the mother of God. Sylvie traces a finger up and down the letter and now the M becomes my future.

'You're going to find a really nice girl,' she says. 'A much better person than me.'

'I don't want anyone else.'

'You'll fall in love with her and she'll love you just as much. And one day –'

'Sylvie, I promise I'll never lie to you again. I'd do anything to make it up to you.'

'This isn't about that, Neil.'

She pauses so that the next words aren't cluttered up with the ones that went before. Her face tells me that the next words are going to be the important ones.

'I don't regret what we did,' she says. 'It will always be special. And so will you. But I love someone else.'

58

It's only two weeks later when Rose marches down the aisle with her dad, their arms laced together. Mrs Smith, the church organist, pumps out the music, all posh and royal-sounding. That suits because Rose looks like a princess.

I'm beside Kevin at the altar. He made me his best man. I wasn't too keen to do it because I thought everyone would be gawking at me – now I know that was wrong. Kevin is much more interesting to gawk at than me. He's got so many butterflies he's about to take off. If he had to ride his bike blindfolded off the Harbour Bridge he couldn't be more nervous than he already is. I'm loving it.

Mum stands in the front row, crying her heart out. Dad hangs onto her hand and pulls faces – he calls it smiling – to cheer her up. But I know it's not necessary. Mum's crying because she's happy.

Probably all families are weird. Mine's just better at it than most.

The music groans to a halt as Rose reaches the altar. In the moment I have to spare I look out at the church hoping to see Sylvie's face.

Father Collins begins the service.

'In the name of the Father and of the Son . . .'

I'm glad they got him instead of O'Brian. It makes a difference when a priest actually likes people.

When he gets down towards the end of the service and asks if anyone has reasons why the marriage shouldn't go ahead, he glances at the back doors as though he expects hordes of people to teem in with their protests. He gets some smiles.

'And do you, Kevin John . . .'

He does. She does.

Forty-five minutes, it takes.

Married.

And by then I know for sure, Sylvie's not here.

We go back to the scout hall for the reception. Soon out comes the food and the drinks, but I hardly touch any of it because I'm too nervous. The best man has to make a speech. It'll be the first one I've ever made and I'm heart-attack material.

Soon I'm up there trembling and raving on, and everyone's bored out of their brains. They yawn through the serious parts, and no one gets my jokes. Mum laughs to try to save me but everyone knows she's just being kind. I'm dying big time. Any sensible person would wrap it up and finish. No one's ever accused me of being sensible, so I keep going – but I stop reading from my notes, and when that happens, I stop trembling.

I tell them about Kevin's smelly footy socks that pong the whole house out – 'Did you know about them, Rose?' – and how he snores with his mouth open, and how once the snores were so loud I put one of his socks in his mouth and the smell almost killed him. I end up with a story that Mum told me. When he was seven or eight Kevin saw a photo of an octopus. 'Mum, Mum,' he says. 'I know about octopuses – they have eight testicles!'

When the speech is over I get a huge laugh from everybody, except Kevin. Strange that. The applause belts around the scout hall like rain on the roof. I feel like I'm a superhero, with jokes.

'Get you later,' Kevin says as I walk past, but he's clapping too, and smiling, just a bit.

For the first time Dad breaks his habit of one home-brew a week. He's downed four or five when he gets up to make his speech. Mum doesn't look real pleased.

'Ladies and Gentlemen . . .'

Good start.

'. . . we are gathered here today . . .'

Struth, they've already been married – you're too late for that one, Dad.

'. . . to wish Rose and Kevin a wonderful life . . . Kev, mate, if she turns out to be even half as good as the old girl – your mum – then you've done well. And Rose, luv, all I want to say is good luck, God bless – and thank you for taking him off our hands. I was starting to think we'd never get rid of the bugger!'

Mum helps him off the stage as everyone applauds. Dad's grinning away, and smiling more than I've ever seen him. There's only one way to describe him tonight – merry.

Whitey Taylor, a mate of Dad's, has brought along a stack of records. He's got the stereo all hooked up and set to go and soon The Monkees are belting out 'Daydream Believer'. Mum bounces up to him, waving her hands like a traffic cop on red cordial. After copping a blast Whitey reluctantly turns it off and instead plays an old-fashioned slow waltz record – the kind people dance to on the night they get married.

I turn all but a couple of lights out and we form a circle as Kevin takes Rose's hand. He's a hopeless dancer but Rose hangs on tight and glides him around the floor and loves him.

In the middle of everyone going 'Ooh, ahh – aren't they sweet', I think of Sylvie . . .

59

The weeks whittle down to the end of the year and then I'm standing in line at Assembly and it's my last day of school.

'Just because you are not in your uniforms, don't think you can run around doing as you please during the holidays,' Mick lectures. 'There are standards to maintain. Whatever you do, wherever you go in life, you carry the honour of this school with you, and you will uphold that honour, always!'

I wish I had the guts to start a slow hand-clap. I wish everyone would join in with me. We'd clap and boo and stomp our feet, louder and louder, and then maybe all together, we could swear our heads off and Mick would have a fit and die, and Delaine would run away and we'd chase him down and each one of us – every boy in the school – would give him six of the best, while we took turns at wearing his sunglasses.

I wish. I wish.

No one dares speak. The last day and Mick still has us under his iron thumb, grinding us down, grinding us down to nothing.

He raves on some more and then he tells us some good news, and some shocking news. The good part is this.

'Unfortunately, Mr Delaine is not here with us today.'

Not even Mick's glares and Clementian on the prowl can stop a rumble of gratitude rippling through the ranks.

'Silence!'

Then comes the part that shocks us all.

'The reason why Mr Delaine is not here is that last night he and his good wife were blessed by the arrival of a baby girl . . .'

That Delaine has a wife – that anyone could love him – that's the shock. And now he's a father.

Clementian claps, uncertainly at first. Mick joins in. He holds his hands above the microphone to magnify the sound, to tell us we *have* to clap along with him. I fold my arms. A lot of us do.

I walk to my first class of the morning with Bails ambling along beside me.

'Imagine someone doin' it with Delaine!' He gives me the big grin. 'Is that weird or what?'

'Nah, I don't think I want to imagine it,' I tell him, 'but yeah, it's weird.'

'But then again,' he says, 'maybe we don't know Delaine as well as we thought we did.'

'You're right, Bails. I don't know him very well at all. I just know him enough.'

'Well, anyway,' we walk up the steps to Mr Wilson's room, 'it proves he's human. That's the scary bit, eh?'

'You've lost me. Why is that scary?'

'Well, he's not a monster, is he? It's not like he just crawled out of the Black Lagoon, Neil. He's human. He's just the same as us. Scary, mate.'

I'm always ready to laugh at anything Bails says because it's usually pretty dumb. This time I just nod.

I'll miss him and my other mates when I leave, but I know I'll bump into them around town, so we don't bother with goodbyes. Why go to that trouble when you can just punch someone on the arm and let that say it all?

I won't see the teachers, though, so all day long I say goodbye to the ones I like. There aren't many that I avoid, and those ones don't care about me either, so it works out well.

Johnno shakes my hand and says he'll miss me. Father Jim gives me a 'God Bless'. And Brother Geoffrey asks if I've done my homework. I start to panic because I didn't know there *was* any homework. That's when he winks at me.

Now, at the end of his class, it's Mr Wilson's turn.

'You mean I won't have the pleasure of your company next year, Neil?'

'Don't think so, sir. My dad says he might get me a job as a painter with the Post Office.'

'Do you like painting?'

'Not much.'

'I see . . . well, don't forget what I told you.'

'Okay.'

I have no idea what he's on about.

Mr Wilson nods and smiles, and forgets me as soon I walk from the room. That's what I think, anyway. But as I go down the steps he pokes his head out of a window.

'Neil.'

'Yep?'

'You have talent – that's what I told you. I've seen it in every assignment you've ever bothered to hand in – and I still remember that story you wrote. You just need to work a lot harder, and believe in yourself. If you do that you can be anything you want. All right?'

'Yes, sir.'

'Good luck.'

That's about the best conversation I ever had with a teacher. It's also the last.

After all the years when the wall clock begrudged every second it gave up, today it streaks like lightning. Our last teacher is Hughie. The hot afternoon gets him drowsy and before long he dozes off at his desk, only to jump up, startled, when the bell rings. The bell to send us home.

60

The School Certificate starts on Monday. We go straight to the Assembly Hall. It's filled with desks set wide apart so we can't cheat. Mr Harris out the front. Clementian on patrol up and down the rows. The subject is English. I've been studying hard. Rose has helped me. It starts badly when I smudge the exam paper with my sweat. But it's English. Mr Wilson's class.

I blitz it.

Every night Mum and Dad tell me not to worry.

'No matter what happens,' they say, 'it's all right. Just do your best.'

Geography and History – Tuesday and Wednesday.

My mates stand around afterwards comparing notes on how they went, checking their answers with each other. I'm smiling.

French and Science on Thursday. Back-to-back horrors.

It's touch and go, but I think I scrape through.

Maths on Friday.

Mum wishes me good luck in the morning. I feel lousy because I already know exactly how this exam's going to end. Luck won't help me.

I go into the Assembly Hall and sit down like everyone else, but for the first time all week I'm not nervous.

Mr Harris takes off his watch and places it on the desk in front of him.

'You have two and a half hours to finish this paper.' He waits for the second hand to hit exactly 9 am. 'You may begin . . . now.'

I sign my name very slowly. There's no hurry because that's all I'm going to write in this exam. I don't attempt to answer a single question.

Only the few people who mark the papers will ever know, and they won't understand why I left the paper blank. That's okay. I'm doing it for myself, not them.

My last small act of defiance.

When Delaine hit me I gave up on Maths, just like he gave up on me. I'd rather score nothing and walk out with my head high than have anything to do with him and what he tried to beat into me. Five minutes after the exam starts, that's what I do.

Outside the hall I run; past all the classrooms and the quad, past the Brothers' house and down Sandy Bay

Road, feeling the breeze and the sunshine, and the tears that spring from nowhere.

Don't know why I'm crying on the best day of my life. Maybe it's for Troy or for Sylvie or because I can't find God, no matter how hard I look. Or maybe I'm like Mum – crying because I'm happy.

One day I'll have all the answers, now I've only got the questions. But that's fine. No matter what happens, I know everything will be all right.

I gulp in freedom, and I run.

Acknowledgements

The writing of *Confessions of a Liar, Thief and Failed Sex God* was helped along by regular workshops with my friends Sandy Fussell, Vicki Stanton and Chris McTrustry. Maureen (Mo) Johnson and Marion Smith were also there to help – just an email away. Chris Cartledge, Colleen and Michael Ryan, and Harry Peters, all gave me valuable advice. As well, I'd like to thank two great editors, Sarah Hazelton and Rosie Fitzgibbon, and Woolshed Press publisher Leonie Tyle, my special saint of patience and encouragement.

Finally, and as always, my greatest supporter has been my wife, Di.

Give Me Truth

I'm an ocean cliff, He's erosion. I feel a large part of me crumbling into the sea, yet somehow I don't mind at all.

Caitlin and David have much in common. They're the same age, they go to the same school, they're both in an amateur play. And each of them is watching their family fall apart.

It's a violent situation, but violence isn't always physical, and neither are threats. In their own ways, Caitlin and David are in it together, but separate. And somewhere, somehow, inevitably, it all has to come to a head.

With *Give Me Truth*, Bill Condon has written another powerful, memorable novel for young people, with characters that stay with the reader long after the last page is turned.

Read on for an extract

David

'I want to go back home,' Allie whimpers. 'Please can we?'

'No one hits my kids. No one.' Mum spits the words out of her like they're made of acid.

I'm jammed in the backseat of the car beside plastic bags full of clothes and boxes packed in a hurry. It's as if we've escaped from a fire and the jumble of things we've saved is all we have left of our lives.

It happened so quickly. They were in the kitchen. We heard Mum's voice first.

'I've had enough! That's it! I want you out of my life!'

'No! It's not that easy! You are still my wife! We exchanged vows! Do you remember that, Lorraine? Do you?'

Allie and I were in the lounge room. I cranked the sound up high on the TV. Cindy laid her head between her paws and puffed and panted. Spit dropped from her mouth and spotted the floor.

'Aw, look at her, David. She's scared.'

'She's a wimp,' I said. 'There's nothing to be scared of.'

Allie got down on the floor and stroked Cindy's head.

'It's okay. It's okay.'

I stepped around them and shut the door but the fight still broke through.

'It's really bad tonight, David.'

'Don't worry about it.' I shrugged. 'Pass me the remote.'

A dish smashed. Cindy jumped up. Allie held on to her. 'No one's going to hurt you, girl.'

I bit my lip and waited. A glass splintered across the floor. In my head, I could see it happening: Mum's face red and twisted, Dad roaring even louder.

'We should do something.'

'Like what, Allie?'

'I don't know. Anything.'

'Just watch the TV. They'll stop soon.'

They didn't stop. Tonight was a fight different to any other. The noises kept on and on. The house shuddered.

Allie looked to me for reassurance. I didn't have any, but when she gave me that look – as if I was the only one in the world who could help her – I couldn't let her down.

'I'll go and see if everything's okay,' I said.

We both stood at the same time.

'I'll go with you.'

We argued a lot, me and Allie. She could be a pain and I guess she felt the same about me. But now, instinctively, I took her hand and squeezed it. It was only for a moment but it was important.

'Come on,' I said. 'They'll stop if we're there.'

We stepped into the hallway. Mum was up ahead. Dad behind her. Moving fast. Both of them. Yelling.

'Leave me alone! I don't want to see you again! Ever!'

Crash went the office door as she slammed it behind her.

'You don't walk away from me, Lorraine! You don't!'

Dad hammered on the door with his fist.

'I want you out here! Right now! Open this door!'

'You stay here, Allie.'

'I'm going with you.'

There were maybe ten steps between us and Dad. I walked just in front of Allie, pretending to be brave. When we got there she stood closest to him.

Allie said, 'Stop, Daddy. Please stop.'

I said, 'Come outside for a while, Dad.'

But he was in another place to us, much too far away to hear. He kicked at the door and broke through the outer layer, leaving splinters and the imprint of his shoe.

'I'll smash it down, Lorraine! You know I will! Come out!'

The door flew open.

Mum: Red eyes and streaks of black down her face. Screeching.

'I'm sick of it, Mike! Sick of you! Sick of this incessant fighting!' She covered her eyes with her hands. 'Please, please – leave me alone!'

Allie ran to Mum and hugged her. Both of them were crying.

'Lorraine, for God's sakes.' Sighing, Dad slumped against the wall. 'I don't want to fight with you – I love you. Can't you see that? I love you.'

'Then don't! Just don't, Mike! Because I don't love you!'

Mum shoved Allie ahead of her, into the office. She dived in after her but before she could close the door Dad pushed it open.

'Lorraine!'

He was rushing at her.

I reached out to him and caught his sleeve.

'Dad.'

'Go – away!'

He spun around and I saw a face I'd never seen before. My head sprang back and there was sudden pain and the room rushed past me and then I was down on the floor. My lip throbbed. I tasted blood.

Mum and Allie leaned over me. Behind them I saw Dad. His eyes were shut and his mouth was open. He was crying. He was screaming. And he wasn't making a sound.

'It's not fair, Mum.' Allie pushes herself back in the seat as far as she can go. 'I didn't even get to say goodbye to Cindy.'

'Not now, Allie. Not now.' Mum stares grimly at the road. 'I have more important things on my mind right now than your bloody dog.'

Allie swivels around to face me. 'He didn't hurt you, did he, David? I mean, not bad – there's nothing broken, right?'

'Nah – I'm good. Fine. And he didn't even mean it, you know? I just got in the way. It was no big deal or anything.'

'See, Mum? David doesn't care. Dad got angry, that's all. He made a mistake. Mum …'

Allie waits for an answer. It doesn't come.

'This is a dumb fight,' she says. 'Why can't we just go home and fix it up with Dad?'

Ignored again, Allie glances back at me for support. I don't hesitate.

'I was the one who got hit,' I say. 'And I'm over it. Completely. It was an accident. You don't just leave someone because of one thing. You know Dad, he's not like that. It was just –'

Mum leans on the horn and the blast kills our arguments stone dead.

Available now